Chasing the Devil

Chasing the Devil

by

William James

Contents

Columbia University-Biogenetics Department   5

St. Petersburg-Russia   9

Washington DC   13

Greenwich Village-NYC   15

Shea Stadium-Flushing-NYC   19

24 Bond Street-NYC   23

St. Petersburg-Russia   27

Bronx-NYC   31

Kabul-Afghanistan   35

Washington DC   37

St. Petersburg-Russia   41

Washington DC   45

Kabul-Afghanistan   49

Washington DC   53

Kabul-Afghanistan   57

Washington DC   61

Kabul-Afghanistan   65

Washington, DC   67

Kabul-Afghanistan   71

Washington DC   73

Kabul-Afghanistan   75

Saudi Arabia   79

Washington DC   83

Kabul-Afghanistan   87

Washington DC   89

Kabul-Afghanistan   93

Washington DC   97

Kabul-Afghanistan   101

Washington DC   103

Middle East   107

Washington DC   109

Hindu Kush Mountains-Northern Afghanistan   113

Munich, Germany-November 6, 1923   117

Hindu Kush Mountains-Northern Afghanistan   121

Munich, Germany-November 6, 1923   123

Hindu Kush Mountains-Northern Afghanistan   127

Munich, Germany-November 6, 1923   129

Washington DC   133

Munich, Germany-November 7, 1923   135

Washington DC   137

Munich, Germany-November 7, 1923   139

Tel Aviv-Israel   141

Munich Germany-November 7, 1923   145

Hindu Kush Mountains-Northern Afghanistan   149

Munich, Germany-November 7, 1923   153

Hindu Kush Mountains-Northern Afghanistan   155

Munich, Germany-November 8, 1923 (7:30 PM)   157

Hindu Kush Mountains-Northern Afghanistan   161

Munich, Germany-November 8, 1923 (8:45PM)   163

Hindu Kush Mountains-Northern Afghanistan   165

Munich, Germany-November 23, 1923 9:00PM   167

Munich, Germany-November 8, 1923   169

Munich, Germany-November 8, 1923   171

Munich, Germany-November 8, 1923   173

Columbia University-NYC 2008   175

"In the Roman Empire it was the sword, in the last century it was mechanized weaponry, in the 21ˢᵗ century it will be bio-technology"

Unknown....

It was one of those hot sticky evenings in Central Park. Everything had a thin coating of water that didn't want to evaporate. The joggers looked as though they had been drenched with a fire hose as their bodies struggled to stay cool.

"Hey Carlos, where is your big date tonight?" asked John Katz

"I don't know yet, but it's going to be someplace air conditioned-like the movies." replied Carlos.

"This terrorist detail sucks" complained Detective Ramos "They've got us wandering around the park like two pendejos; there's nothing going on here."

"Another hour of this BS, and we'll be out of here." responded Katz.

"I'm going to get some ice cream; announced Carlos." "You want any?"

"Na, I'm going to the Met game after the shift, I will pick up a few protein bars on the way." replied John.

Katz watched his partner slowly make his way to the nearby ice cream cart, the one with the huge red and green striped umbrella that was ruffling in the slight breeze.

Ramos's belly hung out like a duffle bag overstuffed with basketballs and his shoulders were narrow and rounded. After seven years, Katz knew one thing, Carlos Ramos was no beauty but was as loyal as a German Sheppard, and as tough as one too.

Ramos yelled over, "Katz this shit is good; you are missing out"—as the ice cream dripped off the side of his mouth."

Katz just shook his head, "I thought this was the week you were starting your new diet."

"It's too hot to worry about any diet—I 'm just trying to stay cool." smiled the loyal partner.

"Did you ever hear of water." snapped back Katz.

"That shit is overrated; that's just big business water companies trying make a buck."

Suddenly Katz's side emergency cell phone began to vibrate.

The Detective slowly reached down to answer it; he felt the adrenaline shoot throughout his nervous system causing his sizeable muscles to tighten.

"Ah crap, I'm getting a call from Chief Molloy at Central." Katz yelled over to Ramos as he devoured his rocky road ice cream cone.

As he placed the emergency phone to his ear, Katz sighed "These calls are never good news."

Ramos trudged over knowing he too would be involved. This was a ritual he and Katz had performed hundreds of times.

"I'm getting too old for this shit." he commented.

"Hey, look at the bright side, at least we'll get some overtime." replied Katz after quickly informing Chief Molloy that they'd carry out the imparted instructions.

Ramos watched John like an old alley cat zeroing in for a kill, his eyes were so focused that he didn't even notice the ice cream running down his hand.

As soon as Katz shut off the phone, Ramos inquired "Now what? Am I going to miss my date tonight and deprive another beautiful girl of this fine tuned physique." as Ramos tried to do his best Charles Atlas while juggling the remains of his ice cream cone.

"We got to head up to Columbia University, to check out some kind of break in at one of their science offices." replied Katz.

"These bullshit white collar crimes always turn out to be nothing but some colleague trying to steal a formula for one of those big pharmaceutical companies." quipped Ramos.

Agreeing with his assessment, Katz merely suggested that they hop on the No. 2 train, instead of taking the patrol car "which would take forever and a day."

"Either way you are still going to miss the Met game." responded Carlos "I don't know why you even bother with those season tickets."

"You got a point there, Carlos." "Today, though, I'm definitely going to make it over to Shea, Pedro is pitching after coming back from that injury."

Columbia University-Biogenetics Department

T he sprawling campus was a beehive of activity, even during the summer months. The eclectic mix of architecture was quite impressive and seems to fortify the mystic reputation of this educational institution.

"Where is the Schwartzberg Biology Building." asked Katz.

"You will need some sort of identification to get into that part of the campus." responded the large chubby security guard.

"We're NYPD detectives; we are here to investigate a burglary." Ramos and Katz stated simultaneously.

"I will need to see your ID's, the bio-lab is a level 3 security zone." authoritatively answered the security guard.

Both Detectives flashed their badges and quickly proceeded to the science building.

As they crossed the campus, they could see the non-descript square building in the foreground.

"It looks more like a penitentiary, then a science lab" "What the hell are they studying in there?" smiled Carlos.

"I do not know, but we are going to find out." replied Katz.

The building was no architectural wonder; it was one of those old school houses that were used at the turn of century. The hallways were quite narrow and musty, common with a building that is over hundred years old. The smell in the hallway was only compounded by the intense summer heat.

"This place reminds me of the city morgue, not some fancy swanky ivy-league college." commented Ramos.

"One term in this place will cost you more than your new car." responded John.

"At that price they could buy some air fresheners." Carlos smiled.

As the Officers entered the reception area the secretary immediately straightened up in her chair. She could sense that they were on some kind of official business.

"You guys are not here to sign-up for Bio-Genetics 101 are you?" laughed the small but genuinely attractive secretary.

As the secretary stared up at John, she became more flirtatious, "What can I help you guys with?"

"I am Detective Katz and this is my partner, Detective Ramos." "We are looking for a Professor Marisa Williams," Katz stated in a matter of fact tone.

"I do not know if she is in the office; let me give her a call."

With the two imposing figures standing at the front of the desk, the secretary had become noticeably nervous and the phone shook slightly as she conversed with Dr. Williams.

"Ok, I will send them right in." the secretary replied.

"Detectives go right in; Dr. Williams's office is in room 258."

As the Detectives proceeded down to the office, their eyes scanned the labs. The hallway was dark and silent. "It's like one of those Halloween movies." joked Ramos.

Katz did not like the environment, the quiet made him very uneasy.

Finally, all the way at the end of hallway, the Detectives arrived at room 258.

Katz gave a little knock and then entered into the office.

As Ramos entered the room, his eyes opened widely in response to Dr. William's breathtaking beauty. This was no nerdy science professor, she looked more like a fashion model, Ramos mumbled to himself.

Carlos shot a glance over to Katz and both men nodded in appreciation.

"Dr. Williams, we are detectives from the 23rd Precinct." Katz announced professionally.

"We have been called in to investigate some kind of burglary."

"Last night someone snuck into my office and stole a file while I went down the hall to the bathroom." Marisa began to sob lightly.

"I have taken so many precautions to prevent such a situation. It was like the person was in the room the whole time, like they were invisible."

"They only had a few minutes." continued Professor Williams.

"Does this data have any kind of street value that someone could use?" questioned Katz.

"That's the unusual thing; I am a scientist who specializes in skin DNA replication."

Ramos blurted out "skin what?"

"You know that replacement skin for burn victims." replied Williams.

Ramos glanced over to Katz, gave a wink, and then a silent "I told you so."

Katz smiled knowing that Ramos was right.

"Dr. Williams is there anything dangerous about this formula?" asked Ramos

No, I am only in the level one testing right now and it will be a couple of years before it even comes close to being put to use.

Is there any other reason why someone would go to such lengths to get into your computer? Maybe it was a practical joke of some kind?

Have you been having any problems with any of your colleagues? Ramos continued.

No! Emphatically responded the Professor "All of my associates are extremely trustworthy."

"Everybody has their price, Dr. Williams." Ramos asserted suspiciously.

"Detectives, this conversation is over." I thank you for your assistance but I will take up the incident with Mr. Deber the department chairman.

"Dr Williams, if you need any more help or if you think of any info you may have left out, give us a call." robotically responded Katz.

"Thank you, Detectives."

As the two officers left the room, Ramos nudged Katz "OOOh!" I sure wish I had a teacher like that when I was in school."

"Keep on dreaming Ramos, she is way out of your league." laughed Katz.

"I am starting my diet and exercise routine tomorrow." responded Ramos.

"It is going to take more then just exercise to win over a beauty like that." answered Katz.

If I move quickly, I may be able to make the fifth inning.

Before Ramos could get in another word, Katz was gone.

St. Petersburg-Russia

Eugeny Ivanson was one of those commanding officers that was feared by all.

With his large barrel chest and massive legs, his physique spoke for itself as he entered the room.

Besides being a physical phenomenon, Commander Ivanson was brilliant, having excelled at the Russian Military Academy in every subject area. Eugeny had risen quickly through the ranks and was now the head of an elite Russian Op Unit. The unit was so secretive, that few knew exactly what the team did.

The beeper went off on Commander Ivanson's watch and he immediately jumped into action. "Make sure those men get out undetected! Eugeny hollered over to Boris, his field assistant."

"Yes Sir" Boris replied, as he watched on the computer screen the elite force meticulously entered their destination zone.

"So far so good." responded Boris.

"What is taking so long?" responded the impatient Commander.

"Commander Ivanson, these are our best men." Boris responded curtly.

Boris's eyes widened like an owl, as he stared at the computer screen.

Suddenly there was a flash of light and then smoke as the team forced themselves into the warehouse.

The security guards were completely surprised as they watched in horror as these creatures in space suits rushed into the room. The first guard who tried to react was shot right between the eyes with the precision and accuracy of an experienced surgeon. The second guard was so fat that his desk stuck to his belly as he tried standing. The guard dropped to the floor wincing in pain from an obvious heart attack. The shock was just too much and the man withered on the floor like a beheaded chicken.

These soldiers were trained professionals and took no chances—immediately shots were fired at point blank range to confirm his execution.

"They are about to enter the storage room, Commander Ivanson." Boris yelled.

The Commander walked over to the monitor and shook his head in approval, "Boris, tonight we will drink."

On the screen the team methodically surveyed the room and moved forward in unison like expert stunt pilots blazing across the sky.

"Field command this is Op1. We are about to enter the room, waiting for approval."

Op1 "This is the Commander Ivanson, enter immediately" Eugeny turned and smiled at Boris like a small child receiving a warm bottle.

"Boris we trained so hard for this mission, our hard work is paying off." Commander Ivanson gloated.

Suddenly on the computer screen, Boris could see the store room door blow into splinters of wood and debris.

"Commander, we have located the target." chimed in Op1.

"Grab it and get out and make sure you make it look like an accidental fire." "I do not want any evidence." bellowed Commander Ivanson "Do you understand Op1?"

"Over—Commander Ivanson"

"The giant soldier returned to his desk."

"Boris, you may be talking to a General soon!" laughed the intoxicated Commander.

"Yes Commander Ivanson, everything went as planned" replied Boris.

"Boris tell the men to return back to base for a little celebration, most importantly tell them to bring the target back in its secured lock box."

"Boris! Remind them that no one is to touch the target."

Commander Ivanson took another swig of vodka and then proudly exited the room.

Washington DC

Professor Harris has eagerly awaited his appointment with Director Cartwright.

I have been painstakingly trying to have the Director implement my theories, my ideas, they finally have listened.

Professor Harris was completely giddy with himself, partly because his life's work was about to come to fruition and partly because of the fine French champagne that was offered in the limo.

"Welcome Professor Harris, please come in we have been waiting for you." stated Director Cartwright, a stately man with the strict posterior of a military lifer.

"Would you like a drink Professor?" Cartwright politely offered

"No I am fine." replied Harris.

"Do you know why we sent for you Dr. Harris?" asked Cartwright.

"I am assuming that it is in reference to my latest article of molecular fusion."

"Well yes that is part of it, but we also need to know who else knows about this project." Director Cartwright asked inquisitively.

"Well there is my team of grad assistants and my colleagues in the biology department"

"Anyone else?" Cartwright sternly responded.

The stressed look of a reprimanded school boy suddenly ran across Dr. Harris's face.

"Well there was also one of my doctoral students." mumbling his response pathetically hoping they would not be able to decipher the words.

"Which doctoral student are you referring to?" "Dr. Harris this is of national importance."

"Do you understand me Mr. Harris?" screamed Director Cartwright

"Marisa Williams, she is at Columbia University." meekly responded the frightened Dr. Harris.

"How involved is Ms. Williams, Dr. Harris?" pried Cartwright

"Well, it was her original ground breaking work on DNA replication that led to my discovery in molecular cell replication in mice."

"Does Dr. Williams know the sequences, Dr. Harris?" inquired Cartwright, who was growing more and more impatient with Dr. Harris responses.

"Wha...Wha...What sequences are you talking about Director?" responded Dr. Harris in obvious nervous sickened tone.

"Dr. Harris, I think it is time you had a little reunion with your protégé."

Men get Dr. Harris on the next jet to New York and let's find out what Dr. Williams has to say.

Harris's legs began to weaken like over cooked pasta when he stood up from the chair, the two gorilla size special agents quickly escorted him to the private airport.

Greenwich Village-NYC

D r. Williams felt her cell phone begin to vibrate in her pocket, she immediately responded like a controlled test mouse.

"Hello, Marisa, this is Michael Harris, I am here in NY and would like to get together." Harris fought to prevent his voice from quivering.

"Dr. Harris what a surprise." Marisa responded genuinely.

"Why such short notice?" "Usually you call or email me six months in advance." joked Dr. Williams.

"You know how anal us scientist can be with appointments."

"Marisa, this is important, I have to see you at once!" sternly responded Dr. Harris.

"Do you remember that little Italian place down on 24 Bond?" asked Harris.

"Yeah I think it was Ponticello's or something like that." recalled Marisa.

"We'll meet me over there at 7:30, and one more thing, make sure you come by yourself." directed Harris.

"Alright Michael, 7:30 it is."

As Marisa clicked off her cell, suddenly she felt a cold chill run through her spine, like one of those winter breezes that seeps into your bones.

Marisa knew Dr. Harris very well and he was never one to do things rash.

The Professor quickly glanced at the clock, the time was 6:00, just enough time to freshen up and grab a cab down town.

On the cab ride down the city lights twinkled on the back drop of the darkening sky, always impressive no matter what time a day, Marisa thought.

Marisa was also concerned about Michael's tone, it was not like him to call so abruptly and talk so seriously.

Dr. Harris was not only her dissertation advisor but a close friend, someone she had always trusted.

Marisa nervously rubbed her hands as she mulled over the telephone conversation in her head.

"Miss, you said 24 Bond right?" "Well we are right in front of it." stated the cab driver.

Startled, Marisa gave the driver a twenty and exited the cab.

"What about change, Miss?" inquired the honest cabbie.

"Keep it, I'm in a hurry."

As Marisa bolted from the car, she could hear a muffled "thank you." as the cab surged back into the heavy evening traffic.

Marisa peered into to window and spotted Dr. Harris.

In the back, behind the over grown fichus plant, Marisa could see the Professor peering out trying to look inconspicuous. Under normal circumstances it would have appeared quite comical but this scenario was just too bizarre for laughter.

Approaching the table, Marisa immediately detected the empty scotch bottle on the table.

"Marisa, please sit down" Harris trembled.

"Dr. Harris what's wrong? I don't remember you being much of a drinker."

"Marisa, we may have gotten a little over our heads with our new regeneration study." responded Harris.

"What are you talking about, Michael?" nervously inquired Dr. Williams.

"Well I was called over to the National Security Agency and they seem to think that our research may be utilized for some dangerous purpose."

"Marisa, they were very curt and it was obvious they were being very cautious." Harris continued.

Marisa, who was now becoming increasingly frightened, sat opened mouthed, quietly trying to digest what Dr. Harris was trying to convey.

"Michael, you mean someone else knows about the sequence that is impossible."

"We took such elaborate precautions and besides how could skin therapy be utilized as a dangerous weapon?" Marisa inquisitively inquired.

The waiter approached the table, and asked if anyone needed anything.

"Would you guys like another drink or are you ready to order some food?"

"Yes, bring over another bottle of scotch" slurred the intoxicated Professor.

"No, Michael, I think you have had enough!" chimed in Marisa.

"Marisa you better order a drink yourself." again slurred Harris.

"You have not heard everything." whispered Harris.

"What do you mean there is more?" nervously responded Marisa.

Waiter I think I will take a martini, called out Marisa.

"Dr. Harris, give me all the information, do not hold back."

"Director Cartwright, at the National Security Agency seemed to think that this info was high level, which means that they would do just about anything to get their hands on the formula." responded Harris.

"When you say anything, you mean anything." cried Marisa.

"Marisa, we are in grave danger, you must get out of the city." suggested Harris.

"Dr. Harris, where the hell am I going to go?"

Shea Stadium-Flushing-NYC

H ey Katz, where have you been?" asked Robert Murphy, the burly, uncontested biggest Mets fan in the world.

"We have not seen you all season."

"Well I needed a break from you guys." smiled John.

Katz thought of telling the guys about his wife but he just did not have the heart.

"Well you have not missed anything, were off to another crap season." responded Robert

"At least Pedro is having a good night."

John stared out at the mound to see one of his favorite pitchers prepare for the delivery.

Katz was always amazed at how these men could pitch so hard, remembering one time having his throwing arm timed at a country fair – a dismal 65 miles an hour.

Cautiously Pedro looked at the catcher, reviewing the pitching cues, and then shook his head in approval.

The powerful man reached back, brought his leg up a then fully extended – the ball shot out as if were blasted from a cannon.

The batter never had a chance, watching the blur enter the catcher's glove.

As the next batter came to plate, enthusiasm in the stadium was growing because Pedro was nearing his ninth strike-out of the game and was in fine form. The crowd was beginning to get behind the pitcher and everyone was on their feet cheering.

"That's the one thing about New York fans; they are loud." thought Katz.

As the roar of the crowd began to rise, John was becoming emotionally involved in the game something he had not been able to do for some time.

Pedro was now strutting around the mound, preparing himself up for his next victim.

John noticed that the best pitchers always have a routine or ritual that they go through every time they face a batter, sometimes it is obvious other times it is very subtle.

It is the formatted routine that leads to consistency in delivery.

Pedro was now prepared to make his delivery, as he raised his leg to generate power, his muscles contacted to propel the ball toward home plate.

Just as the ball crossed over the plate, Katz realizes that in all the excitement, he had missed a message on his cell and it was now vibrating.

As Katz was brought back to reality, he dialed the recall digits and listen to the message.

"Detective Katz this is Dr. Williams, I am at a restaurant down in the Village on Bond St, I think I am being followed, please call back."

John immediately pressed the dial mode and was connected to Dr. Williams.

"Detective Katz, I am afraid that someone is following Me." whispered Dr. Williams in a semi hysterical voice.

Katz had years of experience with terrified voices, this was no over reaction.

"Look Ms. Williams stay where you are and I will meet you down there, what is the address on Bond?" calmly inquired Katz.

"24 Bond Street, right across from the cinema." stated Dr. Williams.

Katz knew the area well, and that cinema, it was one of Lisa's favorites, playing all those foreign films.

"Look, Dr. Williams, I have only one directive and that is to stay in place, avoid even the bathroom." "They will not bother you in a crowded open area."

"Do you understand Professor?" Katz sternly directed.

"Yes, but please hurry" cried Marisa.

Katz stood up in his seat and told the gang that he was heading out for something to drink.

Quickly, like a trained Sheppard dog, Katz made his way to his car.

As Katz let out on the clutch of his Ford Mustang he felt free, he began to run through the gears the car roared onto the Grand Central and began to pick up speed as he headed for the Williamsburg Bridge.

As the Mustang raced toward the bridge, he looked out at the majestic skyline of lights and shook his head in awe.

"This stuff always happens when Pedro is pitching" Katz laughed to himself.

John could feel the arteries of the big city sucking him into the throbbing heart of Manhattan.

24 Bond Street-NYC

As Marisa watched in disbelief as her favorite Professor stagger pathetically out of the restaurant to hail a cab, she suddenly felt helpless and alone.

This can not be happening to me, thought Marisa.

I have worked too damn hard to be set-up like this, I have to be calm.

Suddenly she began to feel like she had to go to the bathroom.

"I knew I should not have had that drink." whimpered Marisa as she tried to take her mind off the throbbing pain.

"Detective Katz said no bathroom." Marisa reminded herself.

As she looked around the small, dark restaurant which was decorated with Italian artifacts and souvenirs, the interior was cramped and romantic at the same time; Marisa realized that no one was standing by the bathroom area.

"I can't take much more of this pain, I got to go for it or I will bust."

Marisa quickly moved toward the bathroom and out of the corner of eye she could see a skinny dark skin man suddenly standing and making his way toward her.

"Oh Shit." Marisa whispered and darted toward the dark hallway leading to the bathrooms.

At this point, Marisa had already made her move and was not going to turn back.

The gangly man with crooked teeth was on a direct course toward her and was speeding up.

Marisa made eye contact, which only increased her fear.

The man had the dark, lifeless eyes of a predator shark.

Like a professional dancer greeting a partner, the man was at Marisa side and directing her toward the back entrance.

Within a split second, the whole abduction was complete and not a sole in the restaurant notice a thing.

Suddenly the bathroom door blasted open and out popped John Katz.

Like a high tech robot, Katz delivered one shot to the head and the skinny man slowly slid to the floor like puppet that had lost its strings.

"Let's move! I am sure he has back up." "Follow me and stay close; these guys are professionals." shouted Katz.

Marisa felt her legs getting weak like a boxer in the last rounds of the fight.

"Marisa, snap out of it we only have a split second to get to my car." commanded Katz.

Marisa could feel his taut muscular arm supporting her as he escorted her out to the car.

As John had predicted there were not one but two abductors waiting in the wings.

Immediately the two men had their guns drawn and were heading straight toward Katz's Mustang.

"Marisa, keep your head down." screamed Katz.

As the stalkers made their way toward the car, Katz let out on the clutch and knocked down the tall lengthy assailant.

As the second man opened fire, Katz could feel the spraying glass rip across his face.

While driving with one hand, John tried to block his eyes from the web of glass.

Barely seeing the road or the assailants, Katz maneuvered his way out of the parking lot and into on coming traffic.

"Detective, who the hell are these people?" quivered Marisa.

"I don't know but right now we have bigger concerns." responded Katz.

Marisa could see Katz's pupils contracting as he concentrated on the oncoming traffic.

The horns blew in synchronicity as the Mustang shot down the roadway in the wrong direction.

Marisa then heard the distinct sound of the airbrakes of an approaching truck.

"Hold on, this is going to be close." directed the Detective with great composure.

John could see the truck starting to fishtail, just like one of those Hollywood movie stunts.

Marisa's mouth was wide open as she stared up at the roof of the Mustang being pulled back like a sardine can and seeing the truck clear over their heads like some massive guillotine machine.

As soon as they cleared the truck, Katz grabbed Marisa's arm pulled her out of the vehicle and then commandeered the SUV next to them.

As the Detective jumped into the driver's seat, Marisa could see that Katz's face was covered with blood.

"John your face is a mess we have to get to a hospital." Marisa cried.

"Marisa, I do not know how deep this thing goes, but we are going to have to avoid the hospitals." solemnly responded Katz.

"Then at least let me wipe up the blood with my shirt." offered Marisa.

Katz's eyes were blurry, but not too blurry to prevent him from looking at Marisa beautiful body as she removed her shirt to make a bandage.

Marisa reached over and wiped the glass and blood from Katz's wounds.

John thought to himself, that it had been quite a long time that someone had touch him gently like his wife used to.

With each wipe, John could feel the pain deep in the muscles of his face.

Tears welled up in his eyes as Marisa had to dig deeper into his flesh to get at all the implanted shards of glass.

With the pain being so intense, it was becoming difficult for Katz to even breathe.

"I am almost done." softly responded Marisa.

St. Petersburg-Russia

C ommander Ivanson's eyes scanned the room like a mother hawk watching her eggs.

"With this type of cargo, no one can be trusted." the Russian giant thought to himself.

"Commander Ivanson, the men are very proud of our mission." shouted Boris.

The noise level in the room was exaggerated by the drinking, and the men were having a great time celebrating their success.

The entire battalion knew that this completed mission was going to mean considerable economic gain as well as promotions.

One of the men came up to Ivanson and thanked him for his guidance.

"Commander Ivanson you worked us incredibly hard, I thank you for your determination because the mission went as planned."

"You are the one who were on the front lines, it was all your effort." cheered the Commander.

As the drinks began to run more freely, the soldiers were now dancing and singing in their joy of Mother Russia.

Ivanson was experienced enough to know that it was crucial never to drink too much in front of the troops.

Throughout the night the Commander ditched his drinks as the men filled his glass.

"I must always have a clear head, especially tonight." thought the future General.

Out of the corner of his eye, Ivanson caught Boris slowly closing the back door.

"Boris!" yelled the curious Commander "Come over and have a drink."

Over the heavy noise, Boris could not hear him and continued his suspicious exit.

Commander Ivanson, out of habit, made note of the time on his high-tech military watch.

"It has been over twenty minutes." Ivanson thought to himself.

"What is Boris up to?"

After another ten minutes, Ivanson decided to proceed to the back room to have a look.

With the heightened state of intoxication, the soldiers hardly noticed the massive man cutting across the room.

With the agility of a trained gymnast, the Commander quietly moved his large frame through the storage room door.

"The dark, damp room reminded him of the musty caves he had to search when he served in Afghanistan"

Suddenly Ivanson's mouth opened wide like a fish starving for oxygen.

With the flickering of a small military type flashlight, Eugeny could see the distorted silhouette of his faithful assistant trying to open the crate.

Like a venomous snake, the Commander's hand reacted with split second precision.

Ivanson instantly fired off a single shot from his M-14 silencer.

Before Eugeny could return his gun to its holster, Boris laid motionless on the floor.

Ivanson knew that the mystery of the box could tempt any man.

"It is going to be a long night." mumbled the exhausted Commander "Boris may not be the only corpse by first light."

Bronx-NYC

J ohn, I need access to a computer, I have to find out what is going on." inquired Marisa as she tried not to stare at Katz's facial wounds.

"At this point, Marisa we can not go back to our normal worlds." John responded with a raspy voice with a hint of genuine concern.

"This is some high level shit and I do not know how far they will go to get us." complained John.

"It is like my whole world has been turned upside down in a matter of a few hours."

"I think the less we try to communicate, the better our chances will be for going undetected." suggested the exhausted Officer.

"Look, my partner has a place over in Morning Heights, if we can get in before they get to him, maybe we could get on to his computer?" suggested Katz.

"That's an awful big if, John." doubtingly responded Marisa.

"I do not think we have any better options, do you."

Katz could see that Marisa's eyes were starting to swell up and began to feel sorry for the Professor.

"Marisa, I know this is a crazy situation but we have to stay clear minded at this point because obviously there is quite a bounty out on our heads."

"John, who the hell would need me that badly?" "I am just a college professor."

"Marisa, you must be connected to someone or have been involved in something that is extremely important."

"Look John, like I told you at our first meeting my research is in skin replication."

"Maybe some foreign leader has a bad case of acne." smiled Marisa.

"Hey watch with the face jokes, I look like Freddie Kruger with these cuts," John strained to smile.

"John can we trust your partner?" inquired Marisa.

"Carlos would take a bullet for me." coolly replied John.

"We have been through some heavy stuff over the years—his loyalty has never faltered." explained John.

"I am just asking, covering every angle."

"You know us scientists, analytical by nature." Marisa responded emphatically.

"If we approach the apartment and it is crawling with surveillance, we will have to abort, so be ready." John explained.

"Damn John you are very thorough, you got everything covered and some."

"Do you think the Pope will be there to greet us?" Marisa mused.

"Marisa, this is very serious, you have to pay attention." replied John.

"These guys are obviously professionals, and will stop at nothing—I mean nothing!"

"We're approaching the area now." "Stay Alert!"

"I am getting a bad feeling about this." John stated cautiously.

"Over the years as a cop, I really have developed this sense of danger."

"It has saved me and Ramos many times."

"Watch out John!" screamed Marisa.

"Marisa get down" commanded Detective Katz

Out of the corner of his eye, like an eagle scanning its surroundings, John spotted a car speeding out of the side driveway.

"Ah Shit! John screamed has he halted his vehicle."

"Marisa they are behind us as well. Stay down." sternly Katz ordered.

"John they are along side the truck." cried Marisa.

"These guys are good." marveled the experienced cop.

"Marisa, prepare for the worst."

Before John could get the SUV into reverse, there were men surrounding them.

"Marisa these guys look like some kind of Para-military" John whispered astonishingly.

"Stay in the vehicle—you have nowhere to go." ordered the field officer in a deep baritone voice.

"Stay calm, we are here for your protection—we're Federal Agents." the field op explained.

John could feel the tension in his abdomen suddenly subside; he removed his hand from his revolver.

"John you think they are for real?" asked Marisa.

"I do not know, but what choice do we have." "They have us cornered." John solemnly explained.

With a sudden crash, John felt the SUV rock as the team began drilling the doors of the vehicle shut with what appeared to be giant riveting guns.

The activity had the look of a pit crew at Indianapolis—with the same accuracy and synchronicity.

"These guys are not playing—they are bolting us in and transferring by tow." John explained.

"They only go to such lengths with contaminates, terrorists, or explosive weapons"

As quick as the SUV was bolted in—they were whisked on to a flat bed truck.

"John what is that clicking noise?" inquired Marisa.

Before John could respond, he glanced over at Marisa— she was already falling asleep.

"Damn gas." John mumbled as he too fell into a deep sleep...

Kabul-Afghanistan

A llah is great." Mohammed chanted as he fired off an email. "The Russian military can be very efficient when they want to be." thought the little gnome of a man.

"It is almost unbelievable that they were able to locate the package." giggled the tiny misshapen creature.

"Soon I can leave this god forsaken hell hole." "Allah has guided us."

"Just as Allah guided us on 9/11." he declared with pride.

As Mohammed scanned his apartment he could see the filth around the room.

The room appeared to be ransacked and smelled of defecation and urine.

Rats the size of cats, rummaged through the kitchen garbage.

"Take that you disgusting creatures!" cried out the troll.

The rats barely flinched as the book slammed above their head.

One of rats glared over as to say "You are next."

"It has been two long years stuck in this apartment" whimpered Mohammed.

"I have dedicated my entire life to this cause. It must come to fruition."

"I have lived the life of a monk, given up everything." Mohammed whispered.

"Allah is great."

Washington DC

J ohn can you hear me." Marisa whispered in John's ear.

"Marisa, where the are we?" John responded as he tried to get his bearings.

"I think we are in some kind of a hospital." "Your face has been completely restored."

"What!" "Get me a mirror or something." John requested in amazement.

"John, I have been in a lot of hospitals but I have never seen anything like this." Marisa responded in awe, like a small child in a candy store.

Marisa reached over to touch John's face.

"John this is unbelievable, not one scar."

Katz enjoyed Marisa's touch and affection

"Marisa you have very soft hands." John responded.

"Well it's not like I am a day laborer or anything." joked Marisa.

"If these are our people, why did they go to such lengths to capture us?" asked the inquisitive Detective

"Maybe because they did not want us to do anything stupid in a panic state." Marisa hypothesized.

"That is a very good answer! You should have been in law enforcement" smiled Katz.

Suddenly the massive doors whisked open, an agent walked in like he was doing some kind of military parade march.

"John, I'm Will Bennet, from the National Security Agency."

Katz's felt a surge of relief; at least we are in friendly territory.

"What is this?" "Are we being detained?" "What was with the gas?" Katz's blurted like he was having some kind of seizure.

"I need both of you to stay calm." directed Bennet—who had movie star looks and spoke in very careful direct tones.

Katz could tell immediately that this man was ultra professional in appearance and in technique, probably a West Point grad – Special Forces.

"You both have been through a tremendous amount of stress." continued the Special Agent.

"Why do you need us?" chimed in Marisa.

"I'm going to get to that, but first we need you to understand the importance and magnitude of this situation."

"Are you sure this is not some case of mistaken identity." Marisa added.

"I am a college professor, that's all."

"Ms. Williams, we need you to pull yourself together." the Agent responded caringly but sternly.

"Look, what you are about to hear is going to change your lives forever." he interjected with honest sincerity.

"You've been selected for many reasons—your physiological make-up, your career background in law enforcement, and your psychological blue print."

"What the hell does that mean, you think I got mental problems or something?" demanded Katz.

"John, in front of us we have your complete biographical and psychological profile."

Bennet read through the file as if he was going down memory lane in overdrive.

Marisa began to feel uncomfortable and embarrassed by all the personal information, and shot a sheepish grin at Katz.

Marisa could see John's eyes whelming up.

"John your wife committed suicide at a very early age, by drug overdose."

"According to our records, she committed suicide due to depression and guilt."

"Her grandfather was a concentration camp survivor – Ausweitz 1945."

"The consensus was that she was extremely close to her grandfather and shared in much of his depression and survival guilt." agent Bennet continued.

"Enough." cried Marisa.

"Why are you doing this to him?" Marisa was screaming at this point.

"At least take me to another room." demanded Marisa.

"Dr. Williams, you need to hear this." firmly commanded the Special Agent

"What is this one of these psychological games?" "Are you trying to break us?" continued Marisa.

"Look at John, he is in no condition to go through this!" retorted Marisa.

"Professor, as I explained earlier that this is all part of the bigger situation."

After coming out of a slight daze, John finally spoke— "Tell us exactly what this situation is."

St. Petersburg-Russia

Mohammed, I have the package for delivery." confidently reported Commander Ivanson

"We must make sure that we communicate only on secure lines." Mohammed reminded the Commander.

"Well, you must make sure that the 200 million goes into the Swiss account that we discussed." boomed the massive soldier.

"Their will be no delivery if you do not make good by tomorrow night." "No second chances."

"Is that understood Mohammed?" the Commander sternly inquired.

"Yes! Commander Ivanson." muttered the little troll.

"Soon the deal will be complete." reassuringly Mohammed responded.

The following night, just as planned, the money was moved electronically into the account.

As an added precaution, Ivanson had his people filter the money into several different accounts, making sure no tricks were being played.

After the filtering was complete, the Commander emailed Mohammed.

"The package will be delivered by an associate in two days."

"Good Luck."

"Allah is great!" cheered the little mole like man.

"I will be famous across the world."

"In two days I will have the missing pieces." Mohammed giggled in joy.

Mohammed could not eat or sleep, he was much too excited.

The days passed slowly in anticipation of the delivery.

"Allah please give me strength." whispered the frail, decimated creature.

"Just a sip of water is all I need" the troll retorted to himself.

The effort to pull his body off the dirty infested couch was insurmountable; slithering his way to the sink left him exhausted.

Suddenly like a sixth sense, he could visualize a man knocking on the door.

"Knock, Knock" mumbled the insane man.

"Wake up you little fool" shouted the Deliverer.

"Allah is great." "I did not know how much longer I could last." cried out Mohammed.

"In this box you will find everything you need."

"Make sure it does not get lost." shouted the Deliverer. "Do you understand?"

Mohammed hardly had the strength to look up to the man, with his mind hallucinating, all he could see was the powerful, shimmering silhouette.

"Not to worry; not to worry," Mohammed sped out.

Before Mohammed could say another word, the Deliverer was gone.

Within seconds there was another knock on the door, like the dust cloud of an approaching tornado, the door suddenly smashed down.

All Mohammed's weak brain could register, was the flashing contrasts of the light rays and the toxic smell of gasoline.

"No please, stop." shouted the pathetic Gnome.

"I have dedicated my life to this cause." cried Mohammed.

"I have located the box, pull out." shouted the Intruder.

"What about me?" "What about me?" the corpse of a man screamed.

Mohammed tracked a small lightening fly as it travel to the ground engulfing into a ball of flame…

Washington DC

The silence was only broken by the clicking sound of the sliding doors.

"John this is Chief Ethan Jones, Coordinator of the Biotechnology Department" explained Special Agent Bennet.

Chief Jones was old school, with erect posture and piercing blue eyes.

His exterior was all business, the special agent automatically straightened up when Chief Jones entered.

"John we have a complicated situation here." The Chief began in a straight forward tone.

"Look Chief, stop beating around the bush."

"Exactly why do you need me?" Katz demanded.

"Are you familiar with the writings of Nostrodomous?" inquired the Chief Jones.

At this point John grew even more frustrated and the vein on the side of his forehead began to pulsate.

"What that Russian witch doctor?" responded Katz.

"No, that was Rasputin."

"We are talking about the French doctor—philosopher, who made predictions in the 1600's." Jones continued.

"Astoundingly many of his predictions have been true." the Chief added.

"Come on, I thought that stuff was a bunch of bull shit" interjected Katz.

"All of the research that I have ever seen has always stated that the information was taken out of context." chimed in Marisa.

"Look I know this whole thing looks silly, but if you give me a few minutes I will put the pieces together."

"I promise no one will be laughing after this conversation." sternly the Chief responded

"Our Intel suggests that there has been a sharp increase in interest in Nostrodomus's teachings, especially in Europe and Middle East."

"I am sure that you have seen all the press on the news and internet about the connections between Nostrodomus and the World Trade Disaster." Jones explained.

"Well the next passage in the anthology refers to a powerful leader who will arise in the Middle East."

"The passage mentions the name MABUS." the Chief continued in his robotic like tones.

"Our recon has recovered detailed information on a top secret laboratory 40 miles north of Kabul."

"The name of the project is the **Molecular Analysis Biotechnology Utilization System.**" explained the experience soldier, with a slight tremble in his voice.

There was dead silence in the room, as everyone's brain took a second to process the clues.

Suddenly like a bolt of lightening hitting a flag pole, the group in unison blurted out the acronym – MABUS.

"Unfortunately the information only gets worse" interjected Chief Jones.

"Any idea what is the nature of the project." inquired Marisa.

"We believe that the nature of the program is cell replication."

"Our best guess is that this is some sort of cloning project" Chief Jones continued.

"Who would they want to clone, some kind of a super warrior?" Katz inquired.

"Look, the Intel is very new." "There are still quite a few details missing."

Katz could sense that the Chief was holding back, he glanced over at the Special Agent and he was very tight lipped.

"John, we have reason to believe that they are trying to clone an individual." Jones was now very direct with his words

"Well, Well" John joked back – "who are they bringing back Attila the Hun?"

The silence in the room was maddening, John could hear the heart beat of the Chief accelerate—the quiet seemed like an eternity, but it was only a few short seconds.

"No John—Adolph Hitler."

Kabul-Afghanistan

The Intruder entered the lab, his eyes dilated in awe. His mind could not comprehend the fact that such a place could exist in the middle of the desert.

The level of technology was astounding—the Intruder had a sense of pride.

"I have the package." he sounded out.

The doctors dropped what they were doing and immediately surrounded him like a pack of hungry wolves.

"Allah is great!" "We never thought it possible." the doctors cheered.

"We have been waiting for long, long time." said the lead doctor, a slight man with bent posture and a bald head

"Let's bring the box into our airtight examination room" the lead doctor, Mustafa labored to carry the box.

Like some kind of perverted funeral ritual, the doctors lined up as they escorted the box into the chamber – the contents were obviously sacred.

The Intruder was last on line, and followed the procession into the chamber.

The doctors quietly entered the small room one at a time, the Intruder's heart raced as he anticipated entering the vault.

As the Intruder reached the door way, the doctor in front of him, turned and pushed.

"What is this!" the Intruder screamed.

The door slammed shut in a split second.

Suddenly all became quiet; the Intruder could hear the distinct sound of gas entering the room.

"Open the door!" he pleaded.

The doctors glared out as he withered on the floor—within seconds the gas destroy his nervous system – the Intruder was dead, blood dripping from his mouth due to the spasmodic contractions of his jam muscles—he had chewed his tongue in half.

The chamber was space age in appearance and in technology—the walls and examination table were polished aluminum.

The lead doctor, Mustafa placed a magnetic device in the lock hole—the team was mesmerized as the box began to open.

All the doctors inched closer in unison to peer into the damp, dirty carrying case.

A putrid odor filled the room as they began to explore the contents, some of the doctors tried to block the travel of the noxious gas by putting their forearm across their nose and mouth.

Even with the vile odor, the doctors continued the strict ritual, one that they probably practiced a thousand times.

The contents were placed into what look like a small metallic oven – a giant computer screen on the wall immediately came on and suddenly the team watched intensely as the material in the box was analyzed.

First the data on the screen was like a numerical maelstrom—some kind of math equation out of control.

All of the doctors stared at the screen like they were witnessing a spiritual occurrence.

The silence was finally broken, when Mustafa began to speak.

"Doctors, this is the moment we have been waiting for—Allah is great!" Mustafa shouted as he watched the numbers on the monitor convert into a DNA helix.

Like a swirling tornado, the DNA strain rotated—spinning rapidly as it began to expand.

"Spin, Spin!" the team chanted like they were at some sporting event.

In the right hand corner a small square box popped on to the monitor—all the doctors were spell bound!

Authentic—DNA Confirmed

Washington DC

A dolph Hitler, Adolph Hitler." John mumbled.
"John, are you alright." interjected Marisa.

The room began to spin and John tried to shake off the haze.

John began to hear the voice, the hideous voice that always resurfaced at every family reunion.

This voice stalked his wife's own inner conscious until her bitter end.

Sitting through this painful ritual was nothing as compared to those who lived it.

Always after some wine, the pathetic voice would take over.

"First it started supple; they removed our identity then our assets." Poppa would begin.

"Then came beatings and petty theft, but no one did a thing." Poppa would continue, spilling the fragments of his sole that had been shredded by this experience.

"Next they set us up in Ghettos." "Yet still nothing." frustrated the shell of a man added.

"We have been persecuted for thousands of years, why would this be any different." Poppa cried.

"The Germans moved so fast we had no time to react." "It was all part of their master plan."

"They caused us to become desensitize, numb." explained the sad desperate Poppa.

"When the transferring began, they lined us up like a bunch of sheep."

"No one dared to get out of line; all knew that it would result in instant death, a bullet to the head."

"Every muscle fiber in my body longed to strike out, yet I would not even glance at the animals." sobbed Poppa.

"The Germans had created the ultimate fear, instant death." "These barbarians never failed to use it!" he sternly confirmed.

"The Germans stripped us of all humanity, turned us into ghosts, incapable of resistance."

"They were very clever." continued Poppa.

"Next came the sounds of train whistle, something so benign became the roar of the devil!"

"Who would they select next?" "Would they break up our family?" Poppa solemnly reminisced.

"In the Ghettos, rumors would constantly swirl like a death cloud."

"With such depravation, confusion, no one would listen—nothing was done." Poppa's body would tremble with each vivid memory.

"We boarded those trains without a word, being happy just be alive." "In the back of our minds we knew we were not going to work camps." Poppa would buckle over in pain at this point.

"Trains were a horror of their own, covered in defecation, urine and vomit, not even room to breathe." "Even the cattle got air to breathe!" Poppa would cry.

"As we passed various villages, the soldiers would throw crumbs of bread into the cars to create utter chaos." "It was a game they like to play, so they could watch human beings mutilate each other for a piece of bread." the broken man gasped.

This was the scenario that was forged in Poppa's brain like a red hot branding iron, so deeply that it would resurface often, like a reoccurring nightmare.

Now Katz was experiencing the same torment, the memory continued.

"When the train arrived at the camp, we could hear and see the fire, not of the sun, but of the ovens." "It was perpetually dark due to the ashes created by the burning bodies."

"We were now too weak, confused to fight back, the masses now preferred death over torture." "This was the end of the human's survival mechanism."

"There was also the unfathomable guilt that comes with being a survivor." Poppa sobbed.

"We entered as a family and in seven weeks I was left an orphan."

"The final dagger, the ultimate irony of irony was that the war had already been lost." Poppa would quiver in his chair.

Katz was coming out of the haze now, Marisa was standing over him.

"John we have to get you back in bed."

Katz was still mumbling, "It was already lost" "It was already lost...

Kabul-Afghanistan

Mustafa's subconscious suddenly drifted back to those dark memories that have haunted him his entire life.

"Move, Move, there is little time"

"You must get inside, look in every room, we want him dead or alive." he recalled the Squad Leader's scream.

Everything had happened so fast, it was hard for Mustafa to bring up the memory - like an antiquated computer; Mustafa's mind struggled to restore the data.

"It was raining—like the flood gates were opened, streets became little rivers" slowly the Doctor recalled.

"I will never forget the darkness in the sky." "Bodies just floating along like trash."

"It was like we entered into another dimension in time."

Mustafa knew that this was a very secret operation, only the best were chosen—he was proud to be involved in such an important mission.

The team proceeded in unison as they entered the bunker.

"The darkness in the bunker was surreal, like being in a deep subterranean cave." "The odor was also very intense."

"A combination of flesh and gasoline." Mustafa reminisced.

"The Squad Leader never told us about the details."

"The training was extremely intense" Mustafa's heart rate was beginning to accelerate just by thinking about the torturous exercises.

"As the men proceeded deeper into the abyss—the light waves of their flashlight shook nervously as they tried to navigate the tomb, creating a kind of grotesque creature on the stone walls."

The trained warrior's facial expressions were distorted in anticipation. Mustafa had never seen such terror.

Even though it had been more then fifty years, he could still see the ghostly expressions on the troops faces, Mustafa tried to shake it off – like Pandora's box, once opened it would not shut.

The visions kept flooding in, Mustafa tried to maintain his composure by gripping the edge of the operation table.

"Doctor, are you OK?" asked his assistant.

"I am alright, get me some water." replied Mustafa nervously.

"You are sweating profusely." responded his most faithful partner.

"It's a little hot in this lab that is all; now get me something to drink." Mustafa replied.

The flashback continued – deeper and deeper they crept.

"The eyes of the soldiers were strained as they tried to look for traps." "It was extremely quiet."

"The air was stale and lifeless."

"The blueprint of the bunker had been quite accurate, the recon had paid off." recalled Mustafa.

Finally the Squad Leader began directing the team to room number 5 – within seconds they were in a vault like tomb.

The ceiling light gently moved to highlight the macabre scene, the bodies were slumped on the floor—rigor mortis had left the bodies twisted and distorted which added to the disturbing vision.

With laser sharp coordination, the team picked up the bodies and began to retreat in the dark.

"In the empty darkness, all hell broke out."

Mustafa was now feeling nauseated from the horrific flashback.

The muscles in Mustafa's face grew tight in anticipation of the final vision, the one that he tried to suppress. The haunting memory was now becoming crystal clear.

A terrific explosion caused a brilliant flash of light throughout the bunker. Suddenly there was an intense pain in his lower limb—Mustafa looked down, half of his calf had been ripped away and was wiggling on the floor like a severed eel.

Like some kind of spontaneous reenactment of the incident, Mustafa felled to his knees.

Washington DC

John grasped the end of the bed, his large triceps supporting his fall.

The memory had sapped every last bit of strength from his formidable frame.

"John, are you alright?" asked Marisa as she supported him on the bed

"Yes, I am Ok?" whispered the Detective.

Marisa noticed tears in his eyes from deep resentment and grief.

Marisa felt her own venerability, her own oppressed inner turmoil.

Thinking about her own experiences growing up in the Deep South with racism flowing freely like some kind of malignant cancer – Marisa was also hardened.

"What do you mean you are applying to Harvard." questioned the guidance counselor.

"Well, I have all the grades and recommendations." replied Marisa.

"What about money, where is black girl like you going to get that kind of money?" inquired the counselor.

Marisa's eyes welled as she thought about all the days and nights her mother had sacrificed, working sometimes two to three jobs just to pay the rent.

"I was hoping for a scholarship?" Marisa answered.

"What scholarship?" "You know we only have four, and you were not selected."

"You are a beautiful girl, did you ever think of trade school." she continued.

Marisa felt completely lost, this was to be the way out—she had worked extremely hard to get the grades and now she was being ridiculed.

"Send the application in, I will worry about the money down the road." snapped Marisa.

"This incident was just the tip of the iceberg" Marisa thought.

Through her entire life, it has been a struggle—racism was a web that surrounded her soul and suffocated her being.

"Marisa, you must rise above!" her mother would respond.

"But what if no one gives me the balloon?" Marisa would cry.

It all came to a head when coming home from a graduation party a group of skin head white boys tried to rape her.

No one came to her aid—she only escaped by her own athleticism and internal spirit.

When she returned home, her mother was terrified—fearing retaliation.

"Please lord, help my daughter find the way." cried her Mother desperately.

The next day the letter arrived from Harvard University.

The experience formed an indestructible foundation and work ethic that would carry Marisa throughout every bout of racism.

The racism also created a cocoon for which Marisa used to protect herself from further abuse, this protective barrier worked quite effectively especially with men.

Marisa knew she had trust issues with men, but deep down she was beginning to feel an attraction toward John.

"A kindred spirit" thought Marisa '"Maybe compassion, for all that he has endured."

Marisa was beginning to feel the weight of John's body, and was now tilting slightly.

"I am no light weight" John chimed in as Marisa began to slouch.

As Marisa repositioned her body she could feel his muscularity.

Katz's grasp around her shoulder, gave her a sense of security and strength she had been longing.

"There is little time here." interjected Chief Jones, trying to get their attention.

"I realize you both have been through a tremendous amount of stress." the Chief added sincerely.

"The Cloning is only part of the problem." Chief Jones stressed again.

"You mean there is more to this horror story." John inquired.

"A lot more…

Kabul-Afghanistan

D octor!" the assistant screamed.
"What is the matter?" "I need some help over here" cried
the assistant

Mustafa slid to the floor and was gasping for air.

The other doctors pulled closer to offer support.

Mustafa was still dazed and began to mumble.

"We had the box, it was ours." the little man tried to raise
his voice but it was barely audible.

"It was in our hands." "The Russians ambushed us." cried
Mustafa.

"We had direct orders from Khairallah Talfah himself."

"The task force had been created as a recovery team" "We
were never given any confirmation, but we all knew it was
Hitler." Mustafa continued.

The other doctors showed expressions of confusion and
listened in disbelief.

"Most people are not aware of our relationship with
Hitler, but there were agreements made with the Arabs during
World War Two."

"We were a likely Ally because of our hatred of the Jews and our oil reserves"

"Saddam Hussein's uncle, Talfah was very close to Hitler and formed many alliances that were to continue after the war."

"Hitler was very supportive of our secular pan Arabism." "Talfah offered him the closest thing to reincarnation." Mustafa whispered.

"You mean to tell me that you were at the bunker, before the Russians?" asked his colleague.

"Yes" "We had Hitler in our possession, but the Russians came out of nowhere and grabbed the bounty." Mustafa gasped.

Mustafa reached down to show the doctors his missing calf muscle.

"I was shot right through the leg, and left for dead"

"The rest of the team was wiped out."

"Now fifty years later we are now about to embark on our original mission"

The Doctor was regaining some of his strength.

"Through MABUS, we are about to bring back the greatest leader of our time"

"He will lead us to glory and destroy the Jews!" cried Mustafa.

Washington, DC

K atz could not believe his ears.
"You mean to tell me this thing gets worse?" blurted John as he tried to straighten himself off the bed.

"John, we have reason to believe that some how the information in Dr. Williams research has expedited the cloning process."

"Our Intel has informed us that DNA—abnormalities that have prevented them from completion in the past have been corrected."

"There is a sequence pattern with the DNA markers, in the past they could not be accurately duplicated" Chief Jones continued.

"You mean that they are using my research in this diabolical plan." injected Marisa.

"You had no way of knowing about the DNA blockers, you were working in skin replication." Jones responded calmly.

"Unfortunately, unwittingly your research has helped them." Chief Jones slowly shook his head in disbelief

"Take a look at this latest footage." the Chief directed the spell bound group.

Suddenly a giant TV screen dropped from the ceiling like something out of a James Bond movie.

Mesmerized - the team stared at the screen as it concisely demonstrated the process for human replication – cloning.

The DNA helix was complete, with all markers and sequences in order perfectly.

"But how could they get Hitler's DNA anyway, everyone said that he was burned beyond recognition just inside the bunker." Katz inquired.

"We now have reason to believe that his body was captured by the Russians." Chief Jones responded.

"Furthermore, it appears that recently large sums of money have been exchanged by the Russian military and an Arab Consortium" "We fear that this money was for Hitler's DNA"

"Were did they spot it on EBay." Katz joked.

"John this is very serious, we have reason to believe that the MABUS project is about to be completed" the Chief interjected with a very stern tone.

"Well, if they are that close, why do you need me and Marisa?" asked Katz.

"John, we are taking a two prong approach to this situation"

"First we have an elite recon team working on destroying MABUS."

"The second approach is a little unorthodox" continued the Chief.

"What you mean by unorthodox?" chimed in Marisa.

"Have either one of you ever read H.G. Wells—Time Machine?"

"What?" responded Katz?

"You heard right." Jones painstakingly continued.

"We have developed a method of time travel—Einstein's theories have already confirmed time travel but it was limited to futuristic travel not the past"

"We have uncovered secret documentation that German's also had a program for Time Travel called Genesis—it relied on radio waves."

"This is ridiculous!" declared the burly Detective.

"John the evidence is very clear; it was started in the early 1920's by a doctor named Fredrick Knoeble"

"There were many problems with the prototype" continued Chief Jones

"Many times the experiment victims had heart attacks, strokes, comas from the transition stress." "We feel with the current technology we have worked out the problems."

"Chief, even if we could go back, what is one cop and a college professor going to do with an entire army?"

"John, we are not planning on sending you back to 1940" replied Jones

"Well what exactly do you have in mind?" interrupted Katz.

"1923…

Kabul-Afghanistan

W e must not waste a moment." cried Mustafa.
"We are too close." Mustafa slammed his hand on the table.

"Let's get the DNA samples into the converter, and begin the process." continued the lead doctor.

The group once again moved in unison as they completed the installation process, like a military drill—everything was done to perfection.

The sample was so precious and fragile that the experienced doctors' hands trembled as they handled the specimen.

As the sample was loaded, the lights on the massive LCD screen began to come alive providing a crystal clear glimpse of the entire process—like a secret tunnel to the afterlife.

"Make sure that all the information is coded correctly, there is no room for error." cried Mustafa.

"We are entering the first phase." chimed in the gene specialist

The LCD screen showed a gigantic DNA helix, the molecular tornado continued to swirl faster and faster.

The doctors all held their breath as the computer continued deciphering the information.

Like gate watchers of hell, they stared as they resurrected Satan.

"Phase two is complete" the computer continued in slow, robotic tone.

Most of the doctors at this point had weakened knees, and were leaning on the examination table for support.

"Phase three is the most critical and problematic." Mustafa reminded his men.

"Mustafa, you are covered in sweat, do you need some more water?" inquired his assistant.

"No, let's continue."

The machine began to slow down; suddenly the machine began to flash;

"MORE DATA REQUIRED; MORE DATA REQUIRED"

"Enter the code" Mustafa angrily drilled the computer scientist.

The computer scientist placed his hands on the keyboard with the delicacy of a classical pianist.

The keys hummed as the scientist then opened the gate to hell.

"CLONING PROCESS IS COMPLETE"

Washington DC

J ohn had to remind himself to close his mouth.

"What the hell do you have in mind, Chief? John inquired angrily

"I told both of you that this was going to be an unusual strategy" replied Jones

"Our research department has given us detailed information on the formation of the Third Reich"

"Our supercomputers were fed the information and out came the best possible moment" Chief Jones continued

"Best possible moment for what?" yelled the exhausted cop.

"John we are asking you to consider going back in time to assassinate Hitler before he came to power." Jones quickly responded.

Marisa could feel John's muscles contracting while he tried to comprehend the request.

"Let me get this straight, you are asking me to go back in time and commit cold blooded murder?"

"John, you were selected for your physiological and psychological background" "First, we need a person who will not hesitate to complete the task" "Secondly we need someone strong enough to follow through"

"Chief, how do I fit into this nightmare." Marisa inquired.

"Marisa you will be needed for other reasons, which we will get into later."

"John we have very little time." The Chief added.

Katz was drifting off, back to the nightmare of his wife and her grandfather.

The horrid tales of deprivation and preservation, the living hell created by the Nazi Party

John was sick to stomach, sweating and shaking all at the same time; the sweat ran down the side of his face like morning dew on the tree leaves.

"Why am I reacting this way?"

"I should be jumping for joy." John thought.

Katz was having trepidation—this was cold blooded murder.

All the years of police work did not prepare him for this; his brain functioned on another plane.

Suddenly a vivid image appeared in his memory; the revolting pain of finding his wife dead on the floor next to bed – the tears, heartbreak.

Next came the vision of Katz's work ethic in the gym, he trained so hard yet had no interest in competition and never went outside with a tank top – John had always felt that there was another reason why he trained – like some kind of primordial instinct, a calling.

Marisa noticed the tears streaming down John's face — she shook his shoulders.

"John, are you OK?"

"I'm in." blurted the massive cop...

Kabul-Afghanistan

The doctors prayed.

"With the new computer technology, not only will we be able to clone but we will be able to select any age and transmit memory" Mustafa mused.

"There will be no need for conditioning." "Our clone will be complete."

The other doctor's eyes were now tearing "This is the most famous point in time in human evolution." they continued to celebrate.

"We will now be able to increase hormones like testosterone and eliminate any chromosomal disorders."

"He will be the ultimate warrior." cried the crazed zealot.

"MABUS will lead us to victory over the infidels" cheered Mustafa.

"We have been waiting a long time for our leader to unite our people." the lead doctor continued.

"Let's head to the formation chamber" directed Mustafa.

The team exited the examination area and headed for the formation room, which was cylindrical in appearance and made entirely of titanium.

"The DNA is fed into the processor—the formation unit correlates the information and initiates the cloning process" Mustafa continued like he was conducting an introductory biology class to the highly experienced medical doctors.

The doctor's eyes were glued to the small computer screen on the side which was showing all relevant information as it was being fed into the formation unit.

As the process continued, strain and sweat covered the doctors' faces.

"Mustafa the screen is showing a reading of 12/1 testosterone level" inquired the gene specialist.

"Never mind" the lead doctor bellowed.

The gene specialist put his head down and would not make eye contact with Mustafa.

The atmosphere in the room became very intense; the other doctors knew that they were not to make any unauthorized changes to the DNA format.

Inside the cylinder, in the green fluid, a tadpole size organism was growing in size.

Electrodes on the sides of the chamber were beginning to fire and small electrical impulses could be seen traveling up and down the cylinder.

With the intensity of the electrical shocks increasing, the embryo was beginning to grow larger and larger.

The reptilian appearance of the embryo was diminishing, now the specimen was looking more and more human.

"This will be the first time in history that we clone a human creature to our specification!" smiled Mustafa.

"Doctor—sit down."

"This procedure could to take awhile." warned the assistant

"My adrenaline is flowing, I can not stop now." Mustafa responded.

The doctors worked silently as they monitored the formation of each body system.

The computer read 100% complete as it went through each developmental phase.

"Mustafa, it appears that we may be ahead of schedule," the gene specialist confirmed.

"Allah, Thank You!" declared Mustafa as he fell his knees in homage.

"The cylinder will decompress automatically, once the formation is complete." the computer scientist reminded Mustafa.

"It is impossible to know how the new organism is going to react to the external stimuli." the gene specialist interjected.

"It may be wise to keep MABUS under restraints." continued the gene specialist

"I will allow no such thing!"

"MABUS is our savior, the answer we have all been looking for" shouted Mustafa.

The computer screen began to count down to decompression – 10, 9, 8…

Saudi Arabia

The wind blew sand across the station window and it cascaded off like one of those etch-n-sketch toys.

The men played cards as the storm passed—as it intensified the soldiers tried to block out the harrowing noise and unrelenting winds.

Suddenly the screen above the bunk bed flashed code red – Recon1.

Recon1 was the most elite military force in the world – the best of the Navy Seals, Army Rangers, etc. – the closest thing to X-men.

Recon1 is so selective that their missions are not even documented and they are utilized for only the most disastrous circumstances.

The men eyed each other in disbelief because the storm was at the pinnacle of its intensity.

Paul nodded "Let's get moving."

The men moved quickly and deliberately, they all knew the drill by now, each soldier had their particular specialty.

The door flung open and smashed against the bunker as they move toward the chopper, the men labored as they tried to balance with the cross winds and the massive protective suits.

Since Recon1 was a last defense, these men had the most sophisticated military equipment—cost was not an issue. Even the helicopter a prototype X84 – was the most advanced craft aviation had to offer.

Each man has been trained in advanced survival techniques, the goal is stay alive as a team but if need be, they have been trained to complete the mission solo.

As they entered the helicopter, which looked more like a miniature version of the stealth bomber, they went through an extensive prearranged checklist – Recon1 was ready for anything.

The craft was very tight, with the combination of the safety suits and the military equipment, there was no room to move.

The men did not even noticed - they were too focused on what was ahead them.

Paul, the group leader, listened as they went through the protocol.

When everything was checked and rechecked, Paul finally interjected.

"Men, May God Bless us—this is not going to be an easy task."

The helicopter rocked a little as Paul began the lift-off, besides that, the chopper was virtually noise free.

All the men were trained pilots and usually rotated - but this time Paul decided to take control.

With a big surge into the wind, the craft swayed a little, and then blasted straight up.

The coordinates had already been coded into the cock-pit computer via wireless satellite.

Paul's hand trembled slightly as he read off the exact destination;

Kabul, Afghanistan

"Well fellows, its show-time." Paul announced with his southern twang.

The other soldiers nodded their heads with very little show of emotion.

"Flight time will be 90 minutes, set your watches now."

Paul noticed there was an unusual level of stress on this mission, the men were very quiet.

The instructions had been very brief which means the Intel was sketchy at best.

Recon1 always operated with obsessive exactness, gaps in data meant risk – the team tried to minimize any surprises.

The code red meant highest level of security and the location could not be hotter.

The men knew that they were going to have their work cut out for them.

The helicopter shuddered as it blasted through the vicious cross winds, with all the latest technology the craft still bounce around like a child's toy airplane – mocking them and reminding the crew of the unbelievable force of nature.

Washington DC

Marisa could hardly swallow; her mouth had become completely dry, as if it was stuffed with cotton.

"Chief, how do I fit into this mess." Marisa's voice squeaked as she responded

"You will be Katz's escort." Jones replied.

"Why me?" Marisa inquired.

"When we send John back, we will need someone reliable and strong."

"Someone who has extensive knowledge in human physiology." continued the Chief Jones.

Marisa's attention was suddenly deflected from Jones; she began to reminiscence about all the racism she had experienced, especially with the Neo-Nazi groups and KKK down south.

All the horror stories inflicted by Hitler and the Nazi party, it was no secret that the Third Reich hated the blacks as much as the Jews.

A vivid memory of that news reel from the 1936 Olympics, Jesse Owens winning the gold – Hitler and his henchmen grimacing – "This was not part of our master plan!"

She also remembered all of those chilling Leni Riefenstahl—NAZI Party propaganda films.

Marisa memory shifted to the attempted rape, she suddenly felt nauseous, and her knees were weakening.

The vision of delivering those kicks and punches to her assailants, at that moment she had super strength.

Marisa had not given it much thought up until this point, but now it was crystal clear, it was divine intervention—she had hurt those men, they were beaten to a bloody pulp.

Marisa had blocked out those details, she had blocked out the entire event – now it was flowing freely.

"Marisa, are you alright, you are shaking like leaf" Katz tenderly inquired.

"John, I am ok" "It's just that this a lot to absorb" Marisa continued.

Marisa could feel John's strong hands pulling her closer, she turned her head and placed it on his wide shoulder.

The Chief noticed the sign of affection, allowed it, but was concerned—this was not going to be a honeymoon.

Marisa was an emotional wreck, everything was happening so fast.

"Now on top of everything else, she felt more and more attracted to Katz."

"Chief, just how risky is this mission?" Marisa inquired.

"Let's put it this way, it has never been done before." "You and Katz are guinea pigs." replied Jones.

"Well, you don't sound very confident?" joked Marisa.

"Look, we would not be taking this kind of risk if it was not absolutely necessary."

Marisa felt John's warm body wrap around her, the shaking had subsided.

With a quick glance into Katz's eyes, she sensed his strength and stability.

John looked away because he did not want to sway her decision.

The room fell silent as Marisa contemplated her situation; she felt her heart rate accelerating.

"Chief, where do I sign on the dotted line...

Kabul-Afghanistan

CLONING PROCESS COMPLETE—
DECOMPRESSION TO BEGIN

T he eerie silence was broken by the hiss of an opening chamber, the green fluid drained out as the cylinder began to go vertical.

The doctors cheered for their creature. Yes!

Mustafa could not contain himself "Allah has delivered!"

As the fluids and wiring were pushed aside, the scientist could see their MABUS

It was Lucifer, Hitler in the flesh.

MABUS was dazed; the bright lights blinded his vision.

"Turn those lights down immediately." screamed Mustafa.

With the lights down, MABUS was able to get his bearings, he stumbled forward slightly.

The doctor's expressions turned from exhilaration to terror, they were gasping for air.

As MABUS stood up, it was clear that he had mutated—his massive muscularity was evident.

"You have destroyed him." screamed the doctors

"Now MABUS will be invincible, the Arabs have waited too long!" Mustafa declared in a fit of fury.

As MABUS moved forward, the doctors stared in disbelief.

MABUS turned his head slowly and smiled at the doctors, "Come closer he whispered in a raspy voice." "Come Closer."

The doctors formed a semi-circle around their leader, trembling at the horrific vision.

Like a flash of lightening, MABUS leap forward and smashed the doctors to pieces, one by one he dismantled their bodies—limbs and torsos covered the blood filled floor.

Mustafa stood quietly as MABUS ripped apart his colleagues.

"Mein Kampf." Mustafa shouted!

MABUS stared at the lead doctor.

Mustafa took no chances, in the conditioning program he made sure he put in direction cues.

Mustafa was an expert on sub-conscious conditioning— he made sure there was a fail safe with his new leader.

Once MABUS heard the directive, he calmed down and listened to Mustafa.

"Welcome Great One." Mustafa continued.

"We have very little time to waste." "Let me bring you up to date." the lead doctor continued like a favorite mentor.

"Yes Mustafa." replied the Aryan Giant.

Washington DC

C hief Jones received a message in his tiny ear phone, his eyes shifted slightly as he digested the information.

"It appears that Operation Seek & Destroy has begun" Jones continued.

"This validates that MABUS is being facilitated"

"We have little time"

"Remember when you go back, there must not be any suspicion" "Your window of opportunity will be slight" Chief Jones reminded the team.

"You will also be briefed by the history experts on when to attack." "Remember John there will be no second chances."

"Both of you will get trained in assassination tactics, there will be no fancy weaponry, just a knife to the heart" the Chief reported as a matter of fact.

"If the crowd goes against you quickly you may not get out."

"Chief I understand the risk involved" declared Katz

"What about the time travel?"

"How will this be accomplished?" Marisa inquired.

"We have always known that the German scientists had been working on a time machine in the early 20's, professor Knoeble had already completed a prototype before the start of the War." the Chief explained.

"Recently we uncovered new information about just how close they really were."

"Our Intel confirmed that the machine existed and worked as early as 1923."

"Unfortunately for Hitler, he did not take interest and funneled money to Luftwaffe instead."

"We will be using today's technology, to send you back to Professor Knoeble's lab in Munich."

"In simplistic terms we will be sending your DNA via radio waves back in time."

"Through advances in technology we can now pin point dates in time and redirect the radio waves."

"You probably have heard people talk about receiving messages or music from a previous generation." the Chief continued his lecture.

"This phenomenon has existed for quite some time now, unfortunately it has not been pin pointed until recently."

"Marisa, you will be needed to take blood samples and put them into the transporter for your return."

"We need an expert, someone who will not fold under pressure" Jones was now looking directly into Marisa's eyes.

"Will we be able to transport anything with us" questioned Marisa.

"This is a very new technology; we feel that the safest transport will be naked."

"No weapons, no medical supplies" Marisa responded in disbelief.

"You will have to improvise" responded the Chief.

"Let me get this straight"

"You are sending me and Marisa back in time, with no supplies; no guns and you want us to stab Hitler to death!" Katz angrily replied.

"John, I wish we had a better plan, but we have no choice, MABUS is in full swing."

"What will be the effect on the time continuum?" "How will this assassination change the future?" questioned the Professor.

"Look Marisa, we have to take our chances on a brighter future" the Chief replied sincerely.

"The hell we went through with WWII, and now this inferno in the Middle East."

"I think we are doing the right thing." added Jones

"How am I going to get close to Hitler" questioned Katz.

"Well let's take a quick lesson on German history…

Kabul-Afghanistan

The cockpit computer flashed—10 minutes to destination. The men's' high tech head screens also flashed the information automatically, they nodded in unison.

"It is hard to believe that there is a lab in the middle of this desert" the co-pilot mentioned with surprise.

"According to our Intel this is a massive lab, everything subterranean" responded Paul.

"With that oil money, anything is possible" joked the co-pilot

"The Intel recommends a frontal approach" "I am concerned about booby traps" responded Paul with obvious trepidation in his voice.

"What other options do we have, the lab was built with "*state of the art* security equipment?" questioned the co-pilot.

Paul then asked the team, "Let's take a little fly by before entry; the helicopter was virtually invisible and inaudible— closest thing to a guardian angel."

The men responded one after another, "Let's go for it."

As Paul guided the helicopter slowly by the entry tunnel; he was shocked to see such a massive door, with heavy steel fortification.

Immediately Paul fed new coordinates into the cockpit computer, "more weaponry needed—target heavily fortified – bunker bomb required."

Paul sent the email off, "Let's stir things up a like bit."

Within a few minutes the bomber appeared out of nowhere —the crew watch as the laser guided missile was delivered.

"Direct hit" the entire crew responded in unison.

When the giant mushroom cloud of sand and debris subsided, the helicopter hovered over the target site.

There was a huge hole in the ground, allowing for quick entry.

Within seconds the craft was down and the men were on the move, as they approached the gigantic crater they stopped at the perimeter.

The smoke and heat from the missile impact, was still evident, the protective suits help to keep the men's bodies at homeostasis.

"We need to get to the main tunnel, the cloning area" "stay close" Paul reminded the team.

All of the men had the latest Intel on the lab, but surprises always needed to be anticipated.

Due to the heat and debris, the men proceeded very slowly into the abyss.

The hole was brightly lit by the inferno created by the bunker bomb; the flames flickered to and fro as the men proceeded deep into abscessed desert.

Paul had a sick sense that something was wrong, it was too quiet.

"The bunker bomb did its job" declared Paul as he pointed to the giant hole in the left tunnel of the lab.

"We would have never been able to blow up the entrance; the bunker bomb to the side tunnel was the only way."

"We got lucky, had they built down another 50 feet, we would have been screwed" continued the Group Leader.

"Where is the alarm or security back-up?" the co-pilot inquired.

"I was just thinking the same thing—stay alert" Paul directed sternly.

"If the Intel is correct, we should be no more then 100 feet to the right once we enter the lab" "Watch from the rear" Paul shouted as they crawled into the dark metallic tunnel.

Heavy Smoke drifted out of the tunnel fogging the troop's vision, the lighting was very poor and spotty.

With every foot step, the suspense intensified.

Heavy breathing resonated through their ear phones, both lung volume and heart rate was increasing on their suit monitors.

The men were getting focused and scared.

In the darkness, suddenly a massive hand appeared wielding a scalpel.

It moved in a flash, puncturing the men's eye shields.

The men panicked as the smoke began to enter the suits, their head gear flashed;

Warning—Suit Contamination

"Back out." "Back out." Paul roared.

It was futile; the rear tunnel doors had already closed behind them.

The team leaped forward, leading right to the formation lab.

The lab had been cleared of smoke and was eerily quiet— the men took a second to catch their breath, trying desperately to regain composure.

"What the hell" Paul yelled, echoing through the teams head sets.

Before them, appeared a surreal freak show—there was a bent over little man in a lab coat and a man who appeared to be a muscular oversized version of Adolph Hitler.

The two were enclosed in a giant glass case, like some kind of a perverted holiday globe

"You have come just in time" bellowed the hobgoblin like creature.

"Just in time to greet our great leader—MABUS." the doctor continued.

"It was written in the prophecies, that our leader would evolve, he is here now to take control and continue with the master plan."

Washington DC

L et me introduce Professor Fink, an expert on German history.

Fink was a middle aged man with an uncanny resemblance to Humphrey Bogart, even in his mannerisms and speech.

When he entered the room, both John and Marisa smiled at each other.

"This guy sounds like Bogart" Marisa whispered to John.

Katz looked away momentarily to avoid laughing.

"You guys have your work cut out for you" Fink began.

"If you listen closely, It will make the mission all the easier." Professor Fink continued.

"We have spent many hours pumping data into the computer to ascertain when Hitler would be most vulnerable."

"Some have said that Hitler was invincible, especially after the Claus von Stauffenberg July 20, 1944 Plot" explained the Professor

"The bomb was literally placed at his feet, and the bastard lived" Fink shook his head to emphasize his amazement.

"Let's get down to business." chimed in Chief Jones "Time is at a premium at this point."

"OK, the computer analysis has pinpointed the target date - Munich, November 6, 1923 – two days before the Beer Hall Putsch."

"In the confusion, Hitler and his SA will have their guard down." the historian continued.

"You will be given every last detail of that period; every tiny piece of information will be available."

"Furthermore, you when you arrive, you are to contact an Ally named Aronin; he was part of the Kreisau Circle" a clandestine group of intellectuals planning to overthrow the Nazi regime."

"A close associate is Adam von Trott zu Solz, the famous lawyer and diplomat was also part of this anti-Nazi network."

"Aronin was a Jewish activist, who hated Hitler right from the start." "All his contact information will be supplied."

"He will be instrumental in getting you close to Hitler."

Fink pause for a second, to regain his thoughts and maybe for effect; "Both of you should also know that both of these men were hung for their efforts."

"Remember that this will be a small window of opportunity." "After the Beer Hall Putsch, Hitler was brought into the limelight."

"He earned his strips with the radicals, these men followed and protected him loyally till his death." the Professor continued with his German history lesson.

"Earlier in time would be easier, but unfortunately, the time machine did not work until 1923."

Solemnly, Fink began to describe the creation of a perfect storm in Europe;

It was the 1920's, Germany was recovering from the First World War, the economy was at an all time low and WWI military restrictions from the Versailles Peace Conference stagnated industrialization.

Isolationism was the philosophy of the day; nobody was watching the cookie jar.

Throw in the Jews, who had control of many of the economic and cultural institutions, you have the Petri dish for the genesis of the Third Reich.

Hitler and the Third Reich offered a one-thousand year-dynasty —an answer to the populace's misery…

Kabul-Afghanistan

It only took the men a few seconds to interpret the ghoulish nightmare.

"The infidels will make great slaughter" cheered Mustafa in complete exultation.

To the group's surprise, the freak began to communicate

MABUS began his dialogue in low but stern tones;

"Did you think that was going to be the end of me?"

"There are forces of evil that will always keep the fires stoked."

"Did you think that 911 was luck?"

"Look at me!" "I am immortal."

"This time there will be no mistakes!"

"Extermination will continue and be completed" MABUS continued in a fury, saliva projecting all over the inside of the globe.

Paul and the troops listen in utter disbelief – sweat was running down their confused faces, heat was building up internally due to the punctures in their suits - making concentration difficult.

Their head sets then began to flash rapidly;

FOREIGN GAS AGENT— DETECTED

At this point the soldier's primordial instincts took over; they all rushed the globe in desperation.

One by one they bounce off the globe like flies bouncing from a crystal clear window.

Mustafa was giggling in delight, as the nerve gas took effect.

The men winced in terrible pain, as their muscles contracted involuntarily—it was a horrific end.

"Lord help us!" Paul blurted as his body slumped into rigor mortis.

Washington DC

G ermany 1923 had been recreated with amazing accuracy and detail.

"Thank you Professor Fink" "You have done a fantastic job" the Chief quickly complimented the effort.

"We have to get them over to the prep room immediately" Jones directed John and Marisa.

The prep room was like a high tech baby delivery room, teams of doctors shuffled around them, frantically tying to complete their procedures.

After about twenty minutes Chief Jones entered the prep room, he was moving faster then earlier in the day - "Folks our Intel has informed us that they have lost complete contact with Recon1" "It may be a total lost" the Chief said somberly.

Marisa peered over at Katz, "This is unbelievable" "Talk about pressure."

"Stay focused Marisa; this is going to be quite a trip" John reassured calmly.

"Just like one of those Caribbean vacations" Marisa joked.

"Look team as soon as prepping is done, we need everyone in the transformation room" directed the Chief.

Before they knew it, John and Marisa were being whisked into the transport area.

The area contained what looked like two large metallic MRI machines.

The entire room was filled with computers and LCD screens; the equipment was very futuristic and resembled a giant airplane cockpit.

Lights were flashing and there was a low drone coming from the transporter.

Katz immediately thought of those pictures of the iron lung they used years ago with TB patients.

"Good thing I am not claustrophobic." quipped Marisa.

"After this you probably will be." Katz smiled.

Suddenly the hematologist came over and explained the DNA implementation procedure.

Methodically the doctor took a blood sample from John and Marisa.

"So you both will be prepared" the doctor directed "the sample goes in the analyzer, which was located on the side of the unit."

"Dr. Williams, it is extremely important that it is a clean sample" "You do not want any contamination."

"Is that clear" the hematologist reiterated.

"If the sample is not perfect—transportation may be automatically blocked."

"I get the picture." Marisa shot back in obvious frustration

"You will both be placed into a transporter." the doctor continued.

"Obviously we do not know what the transportation will be like." "You guys are the first."

"The technology in 1923, as you could imagine was quite primitive compared to today's standard." "Theoretically though, the transport should work."

"Doctor no offense, but this conversation is not exactly a confidence booster" John disgustedly responded.

"Look folks, I am just giving you the fact, this experiment is in its infancy."

"Oh yeah, there is one other small detail." the hematologist smiled.

"Remember that when you arrive, you will be in your birthday suit." "Yes, completely naked." "You will have to scramble to get clothing."

"Look for lab coat or something before you are detected." the doctor continued with his details.

John glanced over at Marisa, who was now smiling widely.

"I do not know if I should laugh or cry."

"This is ludicrous…

Middle East

It was all over the internet; **"Our leader has arrived" "Allah is great!"**

The news traveled like a shock wave – the headlines read – **"The prophecies are correct, first the destruction of the new city—now the arrival of our new leader; MABUS."**

Throughout the Middle East, the terrorist groups began to merge toward unification.

Never before had there been such solidarity.

The Allied Nations watched in horror as the "Army of Islam" began to grow rapidly like malignant metastasizing cancer; the map of the Middle East was reorganizing before their eyes.

The planning for the Army of Islam had not been a fluke, for years the terrorist powers have been coordinating their efforts for the arrival of their prophet – huge sums of oil money have been invested.

The infrastructure was already in place; they were just waiting for their leader to take the reins.

The advent of new technologies in communication has made the transition all the more efficient.

Like the spread of locust in a futile corn field, Arabs swarmed to the streets, willing to die for the cause!

Washington DC

Yes Mr. President, I understand the magnitude of this event" Chief Jones had to lower the volume on his ear phone.

"Where the hell are we with the transporter project?"
"You know I funneled billions into this pet project" the President fumed.

"I understand" the Chief responded softly.

"Are you seeing what I am seeing" the whole god damn Middle East is about to explode before our eyes" yelled the President.

"They are both being prepped, once they are done we will begin the process." the Chief continued "Mr. President, I want you to know personally that I truly appreciate your support and that we are doing everything in our power to implement the project."

"You have my word Mr. President that as soon as we are ready—the team will be sent."

"I will call you the second we initiate the transport." Chief Jones confirmed with sincerity.

"Ethan, I do not have to tell you the importance of this mission" replied the obviously concerned President.

"We will do our best." the phone shook in the Chief's hand.

Ethan ran over to the transport room, "We have to move things along" "How close are we to implementation?"

The hematologist gave a slight nod to the Chief – "They are as ready as they ever will be."

"Let's fire this baby up." commanded Chief Jones

Jones called over his two time travelers; "The United States of America and the rest of the Free World thank both of for you for your courage and dedication."

The Chief then paused, showing uncharacteristically deep emotion; "You guys may be our last chance, God bless you."

The doctors strapped the time travelers into their transporters—as they settled in the machines the door on top slowly began to close.

The pods were air tight and hermetically sealed, lights flashed on the side registering all body processes.

Immediately their heart rate and blood pressure began to accelerate.

Once implementation began, the pods began to rotate slowly, gradually the spinning intensified and the pods became a blur.

The computer screen displayed the transformation of DNA into radio waves—each sequence had a built in check point.

As the check points cleared, the pod accelerated faster and faster.

The worry and strain on the doctors' gaunt faces was evident, as the giant computer gobbled up and sorted all the information.

They all exhaled in relief as the program cleared each check point—the team knew what was at stake.

Due to the design of the transporter, the time travelers remained still as the rotation speed reach extremely high levels.

After the DNA conversion was complete, the computer screen blinked; **"Date of Destination"**

The Chief took a deep breath, stared up at the flashing screen and then began to type slowly;
Suddenly the date appear; November 6, 1923
Confirmed!
The Chief duplicated the routine, November 6, 1923
Complete.
The transportation room rocked as the pods reached unfathomable speeds, the lights dimmed from the surge of magnetic energy created by the unbelievable centrifugal force.

Chief Jones felt for his cheek as the pressure caused his facial skin to recede over his jawbone, exposing his front teeth - his hair was sticking straight up.

Finally it all climaxed into a tremendous bang—the entire crew had their hands covering their ears from the terrific explosion.

Then complete silence…

Hindu Kush Mountains-Northern Afghanistan

"Word is out MABUS." Mustafa giggled like a small child. "The western world is in shock."

"They are not believers, great leader." "The infidels will suffer."

"Wait and see what you will have at your disposal." "Mustafa pointed as they headed toward a hidden entrance way."

Built into the side of a massive mountain was a hidden cave, an entire cache of military equipment – it was a huge structure with high ceilings and expansive storage rooms.

As the two entered, Mustafa hit a switch, which activated the overhead lighting—the sequence went on for an eternity—highlighting rows and rows of massive artillery which sparkled like titanium gods.

Everything from rocket launchers, scud missiles to the cream of the crop; Intercontinental Ballistic Missiles with the latest biochemical toxin—Thoracic Nerve Gas (TNG)

Once exposed to TNG—your lungs collapse causing instant hideous death.

MABUS turned to the doctor, "Mustafa you have done well, thank you my friend."

"This time there will be no mistakes." whispered the Aryan Giant.

"TNG is a thousand times stronger then the gas used in the death chambers"

"There are no blockers, no escape—the freedom fighters are doomed!" Mustafa explained with absolute delight.

"This gas is so concentrated and stable, that it is virtually unstoppable" "Our missiles are the latest stealth design, non detectable—Dr. Goddard and the Verein Fur Raumschiffahrt would be very proud."

"The Vergehungswaffe (V-2) is like a bottle rocket compared to our ICBM's."

"They will never know what hit them!" cheered the freaky giant of a man.

"Besides the missiles, we have over fifty thousand suicide delivers, which are willing to expel the gas all over the world." "The Allies will be completely crippled."

"The World Trade Center was like a walk in the park." continued Mustafa with such malice that his hands were beginning to tremble.

"I do not want to wait an extra second." responded MABUS.

"Call in the commanders, let's implement the master plan" growled the Supreme Leader.

"Your wish is my command" chimed in Mustafa as he fired off the encrypted email.

Mustafa then directed MABUS through the cavern of hell, highlighting all the weapons of mass destruction.

The Aryan Giant became intoxicated by all the weaponry, gaining more and more strength and determination as the tour continued.

MABUS and his demonic sidekick were kindred souls, both hell bent on revenge and elimination.

After the delightful presentation, the Great Leader boomed, "Mustafa take me to the command center!"

Munich, Germany-November 6, 1923

C olored lights swirled around like cosmic lightening flies—producing a terrific light show.

Within seconds, complete darkness—suddenly a small white window pane of light began to grow larger and larger.

As the window of light grew larger, pressure began to build-up as the gravitational force intensified.

A popping sensation was felt as they were thrust through the transporter on to the hardwood floors.

Both were disoriented and weak, they slowly pushed up off the floor; Katz tried to focus as he scanned the damp and musty lab room.

It was difficult to see around the room because of the very poor lighting, something taken for granted in the 21st century, Katz thought to himself.

"Marisa, are you ok?" Katz whispered.

"Yeah I'm alright." "I think we may have lucked out, I do not see anyone around." replied Marisa.

"Do you see any lab coats or anything we can use?" asked Katz as he scrambled around the room looking for clothing.

"Try the closet over there." responded Marisa.

When John, opened the closet three large rats sped out - they charged right toward Marisa.

"Oh shit!" "I hate rats." shouted the Professor.

John quickly stepped in and kicked the rats across the floor—as Marisa jumped around, Katz could not help but notice the beauty of her athletic curvy body.

John realized that he was staring and quickly looked away.

"Marisa, I found them."

Katz tossed the jacket over and then put on his own coat, we better hurry we do not know when they are going to return.

Quietly Katz turned the door handle and peaked out into the hallway, which was very long and narrow.

"Talk about a long walk." John whispered.

Marisa also took a look to assess the situation.

"I think the best route may be right out the front door." Marisa responded.

"If we try and go for a window, it may only increase suspicion." continued the Professor.

"We have the uniform, let's waltz right out of here." it's all about confidence, John."

"Now look who is giving the detective advice." smiled Katz.

John thought for a few seconds; "Alright sometimes the most obvious is the best cover."

"Let's go for it."

As they waited for the perfect moment, Marisa cuddled up next to him.

Katz could feel Marisa trembling under her lab coat, the stress level was unbelievable.

"Look, let's take this one step at a time." "OK." reassured John "We are going to make it out of here."

"According to the Intel that we were given, it should be a straight run." "The only place there may be interference is at the entry way."

"Williams are you ready." John continued with his coaching.

"Yes, let's go John." whispered Marisa as she tried unsuccessfully not to shake.

The couple headed down the corridor as if they were walking on land mines, one slow step at a time.

"See, nothing to it." John whispered back as they traveled at a snails pace.

Suddenly like a shock wave, the sound entered their ear canals.

"Good Morning, Dr. Knoeble."

As the sound of those words registered, Katz felt Marisa buckle slightly from her weaken knees.

"Remember what you said Marisa, it is all about confidence." John reminded Marisa as he supported her with his strong arms.

Dr. Knoeble turned and headed right for them; he paused briefly in front of them and then stared directly into their eyes.

Katz did not flinch, he stared right back into the Doctor's eyes, and they were as black as night—lifeless like the gate keeper of hell.

It seemed like an eternity—finally the Doctor nodded to the couple and proceeded past.

Once the couple was outside the building, Marisa had to take a moment to rest, Katz could feel his heart rate just beginning to decelerate and recover, his neck was still pulsating.

"John, I do not know how much more of this I can take." blurted the Professor as she tried to catch her breath.

"Well, this is just the beginning." John joked back.

"Where to next, great detective?" Marisa inquired.

"Let's look for this guy Aronin…

Hindu Kush Mountains-Northern Afghanistan

The command center was a technological wonder, it had all the latest communication equipment, and the level of sophistication was unsurpassed.

There was a huge table in the center and the flat screen monitors surrounded the entire area like a futuristic game room.

At the head of the table sat the Supreme Leader, MABUS and at his side was his trusted assistant Mustafa.

As the men gathered around the table, it appeared to be a meeting of the "Who's Who of the world terrorist groups."

All of the Middle East All-stars were present, Al Qaeda, Hezbollah, Hamas etc.

These harden terrorists gazed out in mystification at their guide—the silence was only broken, when the Great Leader began to speak.

"First and foremost, I would like to thank all of you for your hard work." boomed MABUS.

"Secondly, I would like you to know that your efforts were not in vain." "We are going to continue to cleanse the world of the filth." continued the Great Leader.

Munich, Germany-November 6, 1923

The streets were still quiet in the morning hour; the November chill was in the air intensified by a brisk circulating wind.

As they proceeded through the streets, both noticed an ominous fog that was rolling in. They also noticed the torn decorations of the recent German Memorial Day celebration—Totengedenktag.

The alley ways were quite narrow and dark; they were basically traveling by the slight morning light on the new horizon.

Some of the early businesses were beginning to open; John and Marisa peered into a bread shop as they proceeded toward Needen Street.

The men in the bread shop did not even look up; they were busily working to prepare the morning goods.

"John, I can not believe that machine worked." Marisa whispered as she shook her head in disbelief.

"Yeah, I know this is pretty unbelievable." "I hope we find this place soon, before we are spotted."

"John, I'm freezing, these lab coats are not cutting it" responded Marisa with a slight shiver in her voice.

Katz pulled the Professor closer to him and wrapped his large arms around Marisa's shoulders.

"I hope you do not mind, Professor Williams" John inquired

"Not at all John, I appreciate the gesture."

Both were silent as they continued their walk down the dark corridor, Marisa gazed into the Detective's eyes and smiled tenderly at him.

Marisa had never known what it was like to be with such a strong gentle man, she enjoyed the sensation of security and confidence.

The silence was also intensified by the unknown; quietly both were contemplating their roll in humanity's fate.

Katz wondered about his ability to commit cold blooded murder, even if it was Hitler.

Marisa feared that she may panic and not complete the mission

"It should be the next block" chimed in John, breaking the silence.

As they proceed by a Jewish shop, three boys appeared out of nowhere.

The boys were obviously drunk and heading right for the Jewish store.

Suddenly the glass door was shattered by rocks thrown by the teenagers—glass shards exploded everywhere!

Katz scanned the situation like a hawk preparing for its next prey, but had to avoid assisting the merchant as he got pummeled by the three young wild racist.

Marisa could feel John's arm trembling as he was forced to helplessly watch this horrific incident unfold.

"John, we have a bigger mission." the Professor responded compassionately.

Marisa pulled John away, "We have to get to Aronin—undetected."

"Those boys are no more then fifteen." mumbled Katz.

"Come on John, this is just the beginning." "If nothing else—use this incident to reinforce your conviction." "There can be no hesitation." Williams continued.

"John, we have one mission and one mission only." Marisa was now looking directly into Katz's eyes as if she was a professional hypnotist.

Katz walked away reluctantly in utter disgust, they proceeded quietly to their destination—25 Needen Street.

"I think this is It." the Professor nodded at the number on top of the door.

"Alright, I am going to give it a knock." responded Katz.

After the light knock, almost a tap the door slowly opened—Aronin appeared.

Aronin was a man in his early sixties; he was of medium height and build.

Although on the slight side, Aronin was quite muscular and taut like a cheetah.

His eyes said it all, even though it was early in the morning – his face appeared clear and intelligent.

"We are friends of Adam von Trott." "We were told you may help us." Katz inquired.

"What is it that you need?" Aronin shot back.

"May we come inside to explain?" John requested confidently.

Aronin stared into Katz's eyes, and then glanced at Marisa.

After a few brief seconds, once the eye scan was complete—Aronin spoke;

"Come in, Come in." responded their newly found Mentor.

The apartment was tiny and cramped; it consisted of one room with a small table and chair in the left corner.

It was more like a book store then living space with journals and novels sprawled all over the area.

"How can I help you?" Aronin inquired.

"Well Adam told us that you would be able to get us closer to this guy, Adolph Hitler."

Aronin raised an eyebrow, "How do you know about Hitler." "He is a very bad seed."

"Let's just say that we have also been following him for a while." "Take my word I know what he is capable of." Katz responded and gave a quick glance over to Marisa.

"I have been in this business for a long, long time—there is something especially evil about this one" "I can feel it in my bones" Aronin responded in a spiritual, almost mystic tone.

"I have seen and dealt with many anti-Semites in my day." Aronin pulled Katz closer for drama and effect. "This one has the markings of the devil!"

"Do you think you will be able to get us close to Hitler?" Katz inquired.

"Well as a matter of fact, my informants tell me that there is suppose to be some kind of a rally at the Buergerbraukeller Beer Hall." responded Aronin is his best English.

"I will warn you that he surrounds himself with a bunch of low-life—especially his giant sidekick, Ulrich Graf." "This guy is huge, a former wrestler, he follows Hitler around faithfully like a vicious watch dog."

"I hear the sick bastard can choke out grown men with his bear hands" Aronin crossed his hands and squeezed his own neck for more effect.

"Do not worry." "We will be careful" Katz reassured their new mentor.

Hindu Kush Mountains-Northern Afghanistan

I t is now time to move ahead." MABUS directed his men.
"For many centuries we have been dominated by the West."
"They have played their little games of manipulation."

"They have kept us at each other's throat, causing turmoil and at the same time preventing consolidation" the powerful leader continued.

"Now we will combine our armies and oil" "The Army of Islam will be the greatest force in the world."

"Look above and you will see the master plan." boomed MABUS with obvious exaltation.

Suddenly the LCD screens came to life; all around the rooms the monitors flashed the war strategy.

The leaders were spell bound by the detail and accuracy—everything was covered.

Everyone in attendance knew about the pain and suffering—but they had persevered.

They were all brought to tears, "This is what we have been waiting for great one" shouted Gullah Mohammed of Afghanistan.

"With our new biotechnology, we can now do in a few weeks what use to take years by conventional weapons" MABUS chimed in as the men tried to get their composure back.

"The Infidels will be our slaves."

MABUS used his pointer for effect, showing the path of destruction—Israel will be destroyed, then he pointed to Western Europe and then finally of course the United States.

If a government will not surrender, they will be annihilated.

There was no remorse in MABUS, or by his loyal followers.

"We will follow you to the end, Brave leader." "Till the end." Mustafa began to chant in a slight whisper.

The other leaders joined in on the celebratory cheer.

"Till the end, till the end!" the chanting continued.

The chant continued until MABUS spoke, "There is no time for celebration, we have our mission."

"Remember that the West has the information." "Their best military team was a joke."

"We cornered them like pigs and they died like pigs." screamed the massive leader.

Suddenly MABUS proceeded away from the podium, slowly like a predatory animal he moved behind the leaders at the table.

MABUS stopped behind, Ali Hussein of Iraq.

"One of us has become too friendly with our western allies." the Supreme Leader bellowed as he effortlessly lifted the man from his chair by the neck.

The crunching sound was unmistakable, as MABUS twisted Ali head completely around.

The seasoned warriors looked on in shock, their eyes bulged like mice in a spring trap as the man's vertebrae perturbed from his neck.

Ali's blood streamed from his carotid artery all the way across the table, covering Lani of Iran with a blanket of red.

"Any questions?" smiled the massive MABUS.

Munich, Germany-November 6, 1923

O ne more thing Aronin, it has been a long trip for us."
"Could you help us with a room to wash up and maybe get
some rest." requested Katz, trying not to be too demanding.

"Yes, I have a close friend away on vacation, you can use
his apartment."

"It will be safe." Aronin reassured John.

"We will meet tomorrow to review details." their Mentor
added.

Aronin gave very concise directions to the apartment, "it
is a three story walk up not too far from the Buergerbraukeller
Beer Hall."

"Do not deviate because that area can get quite
confusing."

"The last thing you want is to be stopped and asked for
directions." "That's the kiss of death."

"Try to appear as calm as possible you do not want attract
suspicion from anyone." Aronin warned sternly.

"Thank you." they chimed in unison.

"We understand the risk you are taking." "We know what is at stake." Katz added.

Their new Mentor hugged them both like they were long lost friends.

"It is very sad that a society that has produced some of humanities greatest, Luther, Kant, Goethe, Schiller, Bach, Beethoven and Brahms—just to name a few has become what it is".

"Now they follow this psychopath, Hitler."

"Good Luck, Good Luck." Aronin responded as he inconspicuously directed them down the street.

After a quick nod the Mentor was gone.

Although it was just morning the time travel and anxiety had taken its toll on John and Marisa—cautiously they proceeded down the street in search for cover and rest.

"John, I'm exhausted" Marisa added as she tried to stay close to Katz.

"It has been an interesting morning" John added with sarcasm.

"What do think about this guy Aronin?"

"I think he is a smart, honest man who has seen some heavy stuff over the years." Marisa responded with her best analysis.

"He is really risking a lot, he is very brave to assist us."

"Unfortunately there are few people in this world who look out for the common good." the Professor added.

"I also think that he has the ability or maybe a sixth sense to determine friend or foe." Katz hypothesized.

Before they knew it, they were at the building—it was an old building, even for 1923.

The building was a non-descript brick structure in a relatively low profile area, which was perfect for their needs.

Since it was still early, the building was eerily quiet, both entered with confidence and caution.

The hardwood floor creaked as they tried to make their way down the hall; each step drilled both of them like they were stepping on land mines.

The hallway was quite dingy and was in need of paint.

"Well it is not exactly the Hyatt." Katz joked.

"At this point I would settle for a park bench." whispered Marisa.

Slowly Katz turned the door key, he did not know what to expect.

The door pushed open and creaked loudly as they entered the room

"Well talk about sparse." Marisa gasped.

"I think the door could use a little oil." "What do you think?" Katz raised an eyebrow.

The room was a shoe box with a writing table and a tiny square bed.

Katz sat down on the bed and it collapse to the floor, a small mouse scurried from the mattress as it fell to the floor.

"When we go back, I am going on a diet" Katz smiled and grabbed his stomach for effect

Marisa, at the point of total exhaustion slowly lowered herself to the mattress.

As John reached out to break Marisa's fall, she landed directly on top of him.

Marisa stared directly into John's beautiful light blue-green eyes.

Slowly John pulled Marisa closer, enjoying the warm sensation of her body.

For the first time in Marisa's life she felt totally unrestricted with a man.

Their attraction was only heightened by the fact that they stood in such a precarious situation, like two explorers looking into the abyss of some vast canyon.

Two soles bonded together both physically and spiritually.

Both knew that at this point there was no turning back; they had only each other and destiny on their side…

Washington DC

Y es, Mr. President." "The time travelers have been sent."
Chief Jones responded directly as possible to the
Commander and Chief.

"Everything went to plan." "As you know Mr. President,
unfortunately the German technology of 1923 will not allow us to
confirm whether they arrived safety or not." the Chief reviewed
the details thoroughly with the President so there was no
misinformation.

"Ethan, our Intel on the Middle East continues to worsen"
the President solemnly responded "We have reason to belief that
MABUS is in effect and is already consolidating the Middle East
region."

"He is being housed in a northern mountain fortress in
Afghanistan, the exact location has not been ascertained and even
if it was, our ballistic experts report there is no way to strike."

"The Islamic media is spreading the news like wildfire."
"Have you checked out CNN?" the President's level of agitation
was rising.

"They have an arsenal of ballistic missiles that can travel long distance with TNG nerve gas." the President continued delivering the critical information.

"What is TNG" "I have never heard of it" questioned the Chief.

"This is brand new biotechnology —it is an agent that instantly collapses your lungs – immediate suffocation."

"For God's sake." Jones mumbled as he shook his head in disgust.

"Are there any antidotes or blockers?"

The phone was quiet for a few seconds; Ethan could feel his heart rate accelerate in the silence.

"Nothing at this time." the President finally responded.

"What about our time travelers." "Do you feel confident they will complete the mission?"

Jones was staring out the office window, trying to digest the new information like an old computer trying to sort too much information.

"Chief, are you still there?" questioned the President in an exhausted voice.

"Mr. President these are the best we have."

Munich, Germany-November 7, 1923

A light tap on the door awoke the time travelers.
Katz leaped up and moved quickly to the door like a trained Shepard dog.

"Open up." it was a voice they did not recognize.

Glancing over at Marisa, "Get dressed quick" Katz whispered.

Marisa put her clothes on and then went directly behind Katz

"John, you do not want to keep him waiting to long" she whispered in Katz's ear.

Their stared at each as they made their fateful decision, like two gate keepers of hell, they slowly opened the door.

The creak of the door hinges was magnified by the intensity of the situation.

In the darkness of hallway it was difficult to determine who it was, Katz squinted his eyes to clarify his vision.

Suddenly all was clear, Katz recognized him right away from the pictures Fink showed them.

It was one of Hitler's henchmen, Christian Weber, an alcoholic bouncer who was giant in stature and ruthless in disposition.

"You dirty Jew; you owe me three months in back rent." Weber's voice boomed.

Katz suddenly realized that this was a twist of fate; Weber must also work as a rent collector.

"You are lucky that I do not throw you out on your ass — Jew pig" warned Weber.

John could feel Marisa trembling like a wet kitten behind him.

The Giant looked past Katz and was now staring at the frightened Professor.

"How are you with such a beautiful women?" "Maybe we can make a deal." Weber gave a sinister laugh.

The Enforcer moved closer and Marisa leaped back.

"Back off." Katz screamed.

John turned his head to avoid Weber's alcoholic foul breathe.

The Giant stuck his chest out like some kind of gorilla mating ritual.

"I am the best wrestler in the Rhineland. I will crush you like a flea," Weber responded.

As he lunged at Katz, the Detective grabbed the Giant by the neck and snapped his vertebrae with ease.

Weber was motionless; he just stared back in shock from the realization of Katz's immense strength and the strangulation due to asphyxia…

Washington DC

Ethan reached for the bottle of fine scotch that was strategically place in his desk for days like these.

He was exhausted; his hand shook as he slowly poured the liquor into an expensive crystal glass.

Just as Chief Jones leaned back in his deep cognac leather chair, the phone began to ring again.

"Ah Shit." "Do I pick this one up?" thought the experience military officer.

The phone continued to ring like a glaring siren, grating on the Chief's nerves.

Finally like a knee jerk reaction, Jones reached for the phone.

"Hello" in low tone.

"Chief, this is the President"

Immediately by the President's tone, Ethan knew this was not going to be good news.

He leaned forward and turned on the speaker phone, and then pulled up close to the speaker as if it were a crystal ball.

"Chief, I just came from my cabinet meeting; it appears that the consensus is that we are going to be forced to use Nuclear weapons."

"Conventional weaponry will not penetrate the bunker; they have built it too deep."

"Mr. President, what about fall out?" Chief questioned.

"Listen after 9/11, we have to be proactive, no more wait and see." there was obvious disgust in the President's voice.

"So we are looking at Armageddon." Jones replied with dull ache now forming in his lower abdomen.

"Ethan, I need to know immediately when you hear anything." "Good or bad." the President's tone was even direr then at the beginning of the conversation.

"Of course Mr. President" Jones had tears in his eyes as he shut off the phone—lines of stress forged their way to the chief's powerful chiseled profile as the disturbing information burrowed its way to his heart and soul.

Munich, Germany-November 7, 1923

Holy Shit, Katz." "He's dead." Marisa spoke in a low tone and she tried to read the giant's lifeless pulse.

"What did you want me to do stand around while he raped you?" shot back the trembling Detective.

"Now what the hell are we going to do?" "We were so close, John." cried Marisa as she tried to concentrate on the volatile situation that was unfolding before their eyes.

Katz scanned the room in desperation to figure out a way to get rid of the dead misshapen Giant.

The room was so sparse that there no extra bed sheets or towels to cover him. More mice crept out of the mattress as John tried to rip off the bed cover.

Suddenly like an echo from hell, there was another knock on the door.

Katz immediately glanced over at Marisa "What is this Grand Central station."

"This can not be good." whispered the Professor.

John stared at the door as if it was the actual entrance to Dante's inferno.

After a quick moment in time, the knock came again.

Katz's hand trembled and sweat ran its way down the side of his head like a miniature waterfall, his entire body convulsed as he turned the door handle to hell.

As the door creaked open slowly, John held his breath as if there were explosives about to detonate.

Immediately Katz recognized Aronin's silhouette in the dark dingy hallway.

The Professor could see Katz's cheek contracting back as his face formed a smile.

"We hear you need some trash collection." winked Aronin confidently.

The Mentor came into the room with four football player size helpers.

The men snickered as they looked down at the fallen Giant, all had past altercations with this ruthless man.

Weber's face was distorted and bruised from the unbelievable strength of the Detective.

Each of Aronin's men nodded in appreciation and awe of Katz's power.

"This was an evil man." "He has terrorized this neighborhood for sometime." explained the Mentor.

As if Aronin was giving John absolution, he touched Katz's shoulder very gently.

"We are thankful" "Praise God for your spectacular strength."

Within seconds the listless Giant was wrapped and put into a large garbage container— whisked away like any other foul piece of vermin.

Aronin stared directly into Katz's intense eyes as if he was reading his thoughts "John, we must all make sacrifices in life." "Stay focused, you have a greater mission."

The Detective could feel Aronin's words soothing his damaged inner soul, within an instant he was ready to move on.

"Mentor, lets have a look at this Beer Hall…

Tel Aviv-Israel

The email was sent directly to the Prime Minister of Israel—a copy was forwarded to every leader in the free world.

"Surrender your land or be instantly destroyed."

"If you do not send confirmation within 24 hours, Lablab, a small town on the west bank will be destroyed."

"This is a scare tactic." "They are trying to bluff us." balked the large chubby Minster of Defense

The Prime Minster's stare was blank, like he was in another world, the realization was just setting in—he had many friends in that region of the West Bank.

"Mr. Prime Minister we must not back down to these terrorists." the Defense Minster continued with his tirade.

"Let's strike now while we still have a chance." the Defense Minister was now screaming at the other cabinet members, increasing the stress to unbearable levels.

"Enough." "Enough." responded the exhausted Prime Minister.

"All of our internal Intel and that from Britain and the US confirm this horror."

"They have the nerve gas and the delivery system." the Prime Minister added with the disgust and frustration of a wolf in a bear trap.

"We are cornered, this is check mate." he continued as he passed around the US—NSA report on the Thoracic Nerve Gas (TNG).

"With this new breakthrough in Bio-technology, this gas will cause violent instant death." The Prime Minister continued as if he was delivering a death sentence personally to his spellbound cabinet.

The room grew more silent and dark as each cabinet member received the report, their eyes glued to the article like flies in a sticky trap.

The information was nothing short of terrifying—nerve gas that could be easily transported was extremely stable and caused instant death.

In the past there was always problems with delivery of gas agents, it was very difficult to target large populations.

TNG was a masterpiece of bio-technology, a synthetically engineered gas to kill humans.

Like letting Lucifer from the jar, these terrorist had created the golden weapon from hell.

To make matters worse, it was hand delivered to the most deadly, vile creatures in the world.

Everyone in the room knew that these psychopaths would not bat an eye on using TNG. In fact, mass suffering would only enhance their enjoyment.

The room had become unbearably hot by the elevated levels of body temperature; sweat was now running freely from the Prime Minister's distressed stone face, he reached up to wipe the perspiration with his hand.

This leader was known to be cool under pressure, even under the most critical of situations—today was different.

"Turn up the God damn air conditioner" barked the Prime Minister.

"What do we know about this MABUS" questioned the Prime Minister with utter disbelief.

The door creaked open and there was a sudden rush of cool air from the hallway, with it the legendary theologian— Rabbi Stein entered.

The Rabbi was ancient, bent over from years and years of osteoarthritis brought on early by the concentration camps— many joked of his comparison to Yoda the master Jedi.

"Rabbi, what can you tell us about this MABUS." the Prime Minister gave a slight bow of the head in respect to the great man.

"In the ancient writing of Nostrodomas there is reference to Middle Eastern leader named MABUS" "The Koran has also made mention of a second prophet."

"The Middle East has been waiting a long time for their deliverer." "They are very hungry."

"The timing is right for their consolidation." buzzed the Master in short raspy tones.

"Never before have had they had the economic and technological means to join forces." the Rabbi waved has misshapen hand for effect.

In a moment of silence, the Prime Minister stared at Stein's crystal clear green eyes, thoroughly amazed that they have not diminished any intensity over the years.

"Rabbi, do you feel that they have found their deliverer?" the Prime Minister gave another slight bow of the head.

Like a court room saga that was about to be unveiled, the room was silent, eagerly waiting for the Master to speak.

"My instincts are strong, as you know I have been around a long, long time" the Rabbi was gasping again at this point.

"He is their deliverer" Stein's body shook in the release of this horrid information

"MABUS is the deliverer of Hell…

Munich Germany-November 7, 1923

As they headed to the Buegerbraukeller, the streets were darkening by the gray ominous clouds that hung in the sky like dirty swabs of cotton.

There was a crisp November chill in the air and a slight passing breeze, as they crossed the street to the huge beer hall, part of a newspaper flew in the air and wraps itself around Katz's shoe.

While trying to subtly remove the paper John was bemused by the coincidence.

"Voelkischer Beobachter" "Isn't this the rag the NAZI uses to condemn Jews and Bolsheviks".

"Yes, evil stuff" "Maybe it is some kind of warning" Aronin half smiled back at John.

Aronin did not waste any time, he moved cautiously and quietly like a bat scurrying easily through a deep dark cave.

Swooping from alley way to side-street the group made their way to the beer hall without interruption—immediately went to work assessing the situation.

The beer hall itself was quite large, it was dilapidated and in need of repair, it was basically an open hall with roughhewn tables in rows that appeared to be endless.

"How many people does this dump hold?" Katz questioned Aronin as they quietly entered the area trying not to be seen by any of Hitler's cronies.

"I would say on a good night over three thousand." replied Aronin with a deadpan face.

"What?" "Did you say three thousand." responded Katz with his mouth open.

"German businessmen like to gather here to have a few mugs of beer and discuss politics."

"This is why I feel Hitler is going to try something tonight, three high ranking Bavarian officials will be here to give speeches – Kahr, Lossow and Seisser" Continued the Mentor.

Katz gave a quick glance over to Marisa and whispered "This guy has done his homework."

"How do think he lasted this long" Marisa responded with a raised eyebrow.

Over here is the podium where they will be speaking, Katz looked over and then felt his stomach getting queasy and a slight twitch in his tight neck muscle.

Suddenly he realized that he was standing by the exact table where Hitler got his infamous start.

As John continued to stare at the worn misshapen furniture, the table appeared to take on a life form of its own.

A slight breeze rocked the table to and fro, creating an unnerving rattling sound "The table seemed to be warning them not to tempt fate" thought Katz

"Pay attention John" "This is not going to be easy" Aronin warned sternly.

"These are fanatics" "I truly feel that they will stop at nothing" the Mentor continued with the sermon.

Katz stared back at Aronin "I think I have to agree with you on that one."

Next Aronin pointed out all the exit areas and handed Marisa a very detailed map of the Beer Hall area.

"There will be no time to get lost." the Mentor now drilled Marisa.

"With three thousand people, once something happens—it will be chaos!" blurted Aronin in a loud tone to emphasize the point.

"Now for the low life Hitler surrounds himself with, it appears that you have already had the wonderful opportunity of meeting Mr. Weber." Aronin gave a slight ironic smile.

"He was a small player; the real inner circle is Goering, Hess, Roehm and that monster Ulrich Graf."

"These are the ones you have to watch." "I will have your back." the Mentor continued like a skilled surgeon preparing for the impending operation.

Aronin pulled Katz over like a faithful coach making the big call, "Once you have Hitler in open view take your shot." "Do not look back or side to side."

Marisa could see Katz chest expanding and contracting in deep thrusts like a bull readying for attack.

Aronin stared at his apprentice, "John do not hesitate." "This man is a snake, he will slither away."

"If he pleads with you for his life, drive the knife deeper...

Hindu Kush Mountains-Northern Afghanistan

T he bunker has been built to exact specifications as Hitler's infamous location in Berlin" gloated Mustafa as he directed the men to their rooms.

Mustafa personally escorted the team down the long corridors, the walls were dark and musty and the lights flicked like summer lightening bugs as the men marched to their quarters.

"Gulam this is your room." explained Mustafa.

"I am sure you will find it quite comfortable." added MABUS's sidekick as he escorted the rest of the crew to their location for the night.

Gulam stared into the hollow dark space which was plain by western standards, but far higher then what he has been use to in his village.

Gulam like many of the rest, were Muslims that were brought up in the Middle East then educated in the west—some at Harvard, Colombia and Oxford.

It was a very tight network, mysterious and yet extremely efficient.

They all have suffered from the actions of the West; the sacrifices have been long and hard—family members tortured and killed.

As Gulam placed his small bag on the bed, he realized that it contained his entire world.

"My whole existence in a tote bag" thought the large muscular leader as he tried gathering all the pieces of this complicated puzzle.

Gulam was by far the most popular and the strongest of all the men, he was highly respected for unbelievable strength and intellect; he often attributes his physical prowess to the fresh goat's milk given to him as a child in the mountains of Afghanistan.

Gulam was confused and conflicted, it was a time of great achievement yet he felt hollow like the empty womb of an infertile woman.

For his entire life, Gulam has only thought about revenge and now on the eve of victory his heart and soul have gone bitter cold.

As he kneeled down for his prayers, he begged Allah for guidance.

"Please show the right way." mumbled the loyal soldier of Allah.

Sweat now dripped from his forehead, his hands trembled in anticipation of any sign of faith.

The leader was sobbing like a small boy who was being reprimanded by a stern father.

His chest heaved loudly as he tried to clear his thoughts.

"Why have you put so much pressure on my shoulders." cried Gulam as he reached for the Koran.

The worn book dropped from his thick scarred hands, sliding off the bed.

Quickly Gulam picked up the book and leaped to his feet with the agility of a hungry charging tiger.

He stared momentarily, slowly swiveling his head to the ceiling like a small bird awaiting the mother's worm.

The book pages were bent in the shape of a triangle, with peak pointing to a quote.

"Allah has spoken."

Munich, Germany-November 7, 1923

H ead right back." directed Aronin with a crystal clear sparkle in his eye.

"Walk casually, no suspicion." in a whisper and then the Mentor was gone.

Both walked silently as they headed to their room.

"John I am scared." declared Marisa openly.

"Listen it is all going to work out" Katz responded in a smooth confident voice.

"Why are the streets so quiet, it is eerie?" Marisa continued.

"I was just thinking the same thing." "It must be the calm before the storm." joked Katz.

The couple cruised their way back to the dingy apartment undetected.

Once inside, they both sat on the broken bed trying to make sense of what was happening, what was going to happen?

Suddenly in the neighboring room, a violin began the play, filling the room with an intoxicating sound.

"I am no expert, but I think its Beethoven." John shocked Marisa with his answer

"You're right it is Midnight Sonata" Marisa elaborated.

"Maybe they are serenading us." smiled Katz.

"Who ever it is, they are a Master." Marisa responded with appreciation.

"Speaking of Masters, one of Aronin's men told me a story about our fearless Mentor."

About five years ago his daughter had gotten in trouble with some boy, he kept harassing her.

Aronin warned the young man to stay away, but he refused.

Fearing further retaliation to his family, he sold his prize violin to pay for someone to deal with this kid, the problem was immediately corrected.

Since that time he no longer played, he said he would do it again if he had to.

To this day—even though he is a master violinist, he will not go back.

The whole incident had darkened his love for the music.

"That's so bittersweet, John." The Professor added.

In the background, music continued to fill the apartment heightening their awareness for each other.

Marisa whispered softly in John's ear, "I love you, John."

"Whatever happens tomorrow, I want you to know how I feel about you" Marisa continued as she began to cry, tears streaming from her face.

Beethoven continued to vibrate through the room increasing the sensitivity of the moment—both knew that it could be their last night together.

John did not respond—he used his massive arms to lift Marisa toward him with more vitality then the night before.

Marisa felt his raw intensity like never before; she was use to dating intellectuals within her own educational milieu.

Beethoven played on…

Hindu Kush Mountains-Northern Afghanistan

K ites swooped up and down creating a kaliscope in the sky, all the different colors created a beautiful mosaic design.

Two final kites were in a calamitous battle, the last one standing was the undisputed champion.

On the top of all the houses stood families watching the event, chanting for a winner.

Suddenly the blood red kite made a quick reverse, dived behind the larger black ominous kite.

With a quick snap the black kite was destroyed, the chanting grew louder as the mortally wounded kite swiveled toward the hard unforgiving earth.

The entire village was now chanting Gulam's name.

Gulam jerked up from his bed, quickly checking his racing heart rate and trying to rub the memory from his eyes.

"Those were some wonderful childhood days in his Afghan village" "What an honor it was" thought the Commander.

The dream was washed away by the impending nightmare, like an over worked computer, Gulam strained to separate his thoughts.

He stared at a tiny spider making his way across the dark sweaty concrete wall, as if he had some magic answer for the Commander.

"Was it Devine intervention?" whispered the powerful soldier.

When the pages folded, they pointed to one of Gulam's favorite quotes about a Muslim man who is asked to stay faithful through many trails and tribulations.

"Much like Job in the bible" thought the Commander as he tried to make sense of this coincidence

"What irony! In the West, Muslims are perceived to be blood thirsty but in actually in the Koran it was the opposite" Gulam continued to analyze his fate.

"Would the Koran justify total Annihilation?" "What are MABUS's pure goals?"

The Spider turned, stopped and was motionless as if it were listening to his desperate speech.

"What do you think my little friend?" joked Gulam.

As if it were staged, the spider moved its tiny body side to side, and then dashed into a crack.

Munich, Germany-November 8, 1923 (7:30 PM)

W ell, I now know how Pedro feels before the big game." Katz smiled over to Marisa.

"Yeah, but this is the game of life —maybe world peace." the Professor responded back.

Aronin advised us to lay low till about 8:15pm, we do not want to get there too early and raise any suspicion.

"Fink told us that the attempted takeover will take place at exactly 8:45, hopefully we will be out of here by 9:30" Katz added with a slight nod.

"Yeah but what world will we be going back to?" the Professor became philosophical.

"Think positive, it's all we have right now." John smiled unconvincingly.

"We do not even know if the time machine will get us back." declared Marisa.

Suddenly there was a knock on the door, they both stared at each other in appreciation of what they had been through and the unchartered waters they were about to explore.

Aronin quickly slid in and began his final lecture "Our Intel has confirmed that everything appears to be moving forward." "Hitler was going to make a coup attempt a few nights ago, but he dropped it because he heard the big three were to be in attendance tonight."

"The beer hall is already quite crowded which will help with maintaining your cover."

"My people will have your back, try not to panic." "Just remember that this is a sick individual—a cancer." their Mentor suddenly raised his voice for effect.

"Graf is very strong. Avoid him if possible."

In a final gesture he touched John and Marisa on their shoulders, looked directly into their eyes—God is with you two.

Both had their heads down, tears formed in their eyes as they tried to grasp the magnitude of the crisis.

When they raised their heads, Aronin was gone.

They headed out to the Beer Hall in the dark cold November chill; they were two time travelers trying to correct the biggest aberration in time.

Along the sidewalk, Katz immediately noticed that Aronin had escorts in place, like a boxer heading to the title fight; they were surrounded by a large entourage.

"At this point in time, everything was in place." thought Katz as he felt the muscles in his lower abdomen tighten once again.

John tried to concentrate on the damage these men had placed on his family and the world, all those horrid memories.

Like an ominous rain cloud, Katz could now see the mass of Nazi supporters converging on the Beer Hall, walking in unison like a pack of worker ants.

He realized that Marisa was no longer by his side; they had decided it would be too risky to bring her inside the Beer Hall.

John instantly missed her in his heart, but knew it was for the best.

The entire group flowed into the cavernous beer hall like blood flows through an arterial system – rapidly the room began to fill to capacity.

John moved with the flow and was immediately pushed to the front of the stage.

Before he even had time to catch his breathe, Katz made visual contact.

Right in front of him stood Satan himself in the flesh.

He quickly glanced at the watch Aronin had given him — 8:35 pm.

"Great. Hitler is by himself" thought the nervous Detective.

He turned to look at the other side of the stage "Ah Shit— there stood Graf."

Katz could not miss him; he was simply huge, "Probably over seven feet—350 lbs."

The minutes flew by 8:36, 37, 38…

Hindu Kush Mountains-Northern Afghanistan

A loud rumble disrupted Gulam concentration. Suddenly he realized that the noise was the sound system, directing the men to the command center immediately.

"All men report to the command center." the speaker bellowed

The entire team assembled in the room in a matter of minutes, no one was late—not after MABUS's graphic demonstration earlier.

"Gentlemen, we have not heard from Israel, it is now time for us to start the extermination" MABUS spoke in a stern tone.

In front of him was a high tech wireless laptop—capable of launching missiles throughout the Middle East and beyond.

"All I need to do is punch in the code and Israel is a ghost town" gloated the Master Leader.

The men around the table were rabid; they could not wait for MABUS to launch—many stood stomping up and down in anticipation.

Gulam look up into the massive LCD screen that was ticking down—Time for Launch 8:45 PM!

The command center had the feel of a highly contested sporting event, everyone cheering and chanting.

MABUS stood like all the tyrants that existed before him—waving his hand to his loyal followers "Veni, Vidi, Vivi—I came, I saw, I conquered.

Gulam knew in his sole that this was not the way of Allah—Allah is great!

Gulam's arm muscles began to contract as he bent over to pick up his massive sword.

Munich, Germany-November 8, 1923 (8:45PM)

T his is Surreal." thought Katz as he looked at is watch which read 8:45PM.

Before his eyes he could see the players moving in place like a human chess match.

As predicted, Hitler began to move toward the table.

Like an enraged bull, Katz charged at Hitler.

Before he could get there, Graf moved into action to defend his leader.

Like the clashing of two massive carnivore dinosaurs, they smashed into each other reaching and grapping for control.

Graf reached down and bit Katz's in the neck, pulling off a sizable chunk of his trapezius muscle.

Katz step back to concentrate, trying to facilitate what was taught by the self-defense instructors—"Step back and deliver an elbow thrust."

John reached back with all his strength and then delivered his elbow directly into Graf's face.

The Massive Graf went down like a ton of bricks—trying to restore his crushed distorted nose.

Katz continued with his mission—heading directly for Hitler, who was watching the entire thing unfold before his eyes.

John was surprised at how tiny this man really was he appeared to shrink even more once Katz had him in his grasp.

"Please spare me." "I mean no harm." cried Hitler with a boyish grin.

Quickly Katz's brought the knife up to Hitler's heart but hesitated as he stared into Hitler's satanic black eyes.

"Yo Amigo, finish the Job" John felt another hand on his.

It was Ramos, his partner. "Let's finish this Puta."

The knife shook with electricity as they both plunged it into Hitler's heart. The beer hall shook momentarily as though there was some kind of realignment of time. A sonic boom blasted their ear drums—then eerie silence...

Hindu Kush Mountains-Northern Afghanistan

Gulam swung his massive sword toward MABUS.

Mustafa stood up to protect his master and intercepted the razor sharp sword.

Gulam swung with such strength and intensity that Mustafa did not even have time to react—his head was cleanly cut off his body.

The Master Leader was infuriated by the attack; he gave out a shuttering roar like a caged lion being withheld its juicy meat

"You will die" MABUS screamed as he looked down at his dismembered faithful sidekick—the body was still convulsing on the floor.

The Great Leader leaped over and picked up Gulam from his chair like he was a tiny puppy dog—while the other leaders watched in horror.

The room went dead silent, except for the slight hum of the high output LCD screens.

In a desperate second attempt; Gulam tried to swing his massive sword at MABUS.

The action only antagonized the Master Leader even more—he grabbed Gulam's wrist and snapped it like a match stick.

The weaken Gulam screamed in pain as MABUS continued to mutilate his arm.

On the verge of passing out, Gulam pulled out his worn copy of the Koran, opening up to the folded page.

MABUS laughed mockingly "You do not deserve to read that book" "What are you going to do hit me over the head?"

"Forgive me Allah." "This evil creature does not deserve to lead our people" Gulam mumbled.

As MABUS moved in for the kill, Gulam smashed the book into the monster's distorted face, releasing TNG from a small vial that was hidden in the binding.

The LCD monitor reads 8:47 – the room is lifeless.

Munich, Germany-November 23, 1923
9:00PM

W hat did you think they were going to do let you do the job alone?" joked Ramos as he pushed his dumfounded partner out the door.

As Katz and Ramos bolted for the exit, Graf got back up, his face was a bloody red pulp like a smashed rotten tomato.

The Giant reached into his pocket and pulled out a large butcher's knife.

Out of nowhere, Aronin intercepted the crazed beast, taking the small sword in his stomach.

As Aronin withered in pain on the floor, Graf reached over and pulled the knife out with pleasure. "Take that you Jew bastard." he roared.

Graf then turned slowly like an enraged monster, glaring at Katz "You will not escape."

With a flick of his wrist, Graf threw the butchers' knife with the accuracy of a professional assassin.

A direct hit, the knife sliced deeply into John's hamstring—rendering him helpless as a baby on the hard floor.

Graf then charged at Katz like a raging rhino closing in for kill.

As Graf charged across the room, Ramos pushed the heavy metal table right in his path, stopping him in his tracks – the Giant smashed to the floor.

Ramos ran over to help his injured best friend.

"Carlos, I am not going to make it." "Get out of here." cried John as he winced in pain from the torn hamstring.

"I'm too heavy; there is no way to carry me." "Just get Marisa home." continued Katz as he trembled in pain.

Ramos was now crying, but understood the inevitable.

"You're the best, Katz." mumbled Carlos as the tears dripped onto John's grimaced face.

"Ramos, tell Marisa she did great—tell her I love her." Ramos nodded then he was gone...

Munich, Germany-November 8, 1923

Outside the Beer Hall it was chaos—The German businessmen were trying to exit and the police were pushing in.

Aronin's men directed Ramos to Marisa, who was waiting patiently in a dark alleyway.

"Where is John?" cried Marisa.

Carlos just stared at Marisa, as the Professor fell to her knees.

"Where is John?" Marisa was now looking up at Ramos, tears streaming from her angelic face.

"After we got Hitler, his henchman Graf stabbed Katz in the back of his leg" "I could not get him back." "Marisa, all he wanted was for you to get back home." explained Carlos, each sentence was more painful then the first.

Marisa was quivering in grief as she tried to digest the information.

"I have to go back for him, Ramos, I love him. I can't leave him here." the Professor cried.

"It's not possible, Marisa." Carlos tried to respond delicately.

"We have to get to the laboratory, before they start figuring this thing out" Ramos continued with tears in his eyes.

Ramos used all of his strength to pick Marisa up, directing her tenderly to his shoulder.

"It is going to work out. Marisa"

Carlos wondered with concern that Marisa may go into shock, making the return trip impossible —Ramos was also touched by her genuine love for Katz.

"Damn, it's only been a few days" thought the tough cop "She's already falling for that big fool."

"Katz must be as good as you thought he was." smiled Ramos as he tried to help Marisa regain her composure.

Aronin's men stood a respectful distance away, patiently waiting to complete their mission, which was to get the time travelers back to the laboratory.

Marisa gave one last long heave, and then wiped her nose.

"It never would have worked anyway, Katz definitely snored too much." joked the Professor.

Ramos gave a little laugh – "He was one of those health nuts, he would drive you crazy."

"We have to go." intervened one of Aronin's men, as he nodded to the street that led to the Laboratory.

"Dr. Knoeble likes to work all hours – day or night." "This may be complicated."

Ramos put his chubby arm around Marisa and subtly pushed the Professor toward the laboratory.

As they walked they tried to contemplate what had just happened - fear was creeping back into their bodies like the shock of a cold water bath.

"I hope this machine works" whispered Marisa.

"Well, I hope you do not mind dinosaurs" responded Ramos with a wink and a smile…

Munich, Germany-November 8, 1923

Katz could hear gunshots.

He reached down to feel his hamstring it was bleeding profusely. He tried to re-position himself but he could not move.

Feeling like a cow being prepared for slaughter, Katz made one more last ditch effort to move.

"Stay down you damn fool." whispered Aronin.

The Mentor pulled himself over to where the devil was lying, feeling for his carotid artery in his neck.

"No pulse." "One less monster." thought Aronin.

Crawling over to Katz, "You did well, never look back." "This Hitler was capable of anything."

Before answering, Aronin was gone.

Suddenly John felt big, strong hands grapping his shoulders and legs—with in seconds they were out of the Beer Hall.

Moving through a semi-conscious state, Katz could see and hear voices all around him.

At one point there was some sort of medical procedure, seeing the varying lights as he was moved in and out of rooms.

"You will make a full recovery" the doctor explained as John began to regain some consciousness.

"The room was more like an apartment then a hospital" thought Katz while trying to get his bearings.

"Obviously they were trying to hide me." Katz mumbled incoherently.

John felt the doctor gently closing his eyelids, sleep my hero, you were very brave tonight.

When Katz finally arose, he did not recognize his surroundings, a cold sensation shot through his nervous system.

The Detective then heard an unfamiliar voice. "Where am I?" shouted Katz, still a little delirious.

"You are with friends." the small slender older man spoke from the corner of the room.

"You are a very brave man." the voice added "It is an honor to assist you."

The gentleman passed Katz a small newspaper article—it mentioned that there was an attempted coup, but it was squashed—most the rowdies were dead.

Katz quickly scanned the article for the names listed, he recognized them all but was only looking for one—there on bottom, in small print; A. Hitler.

John put his hands over his face and for the very the first time began to sob; his emotions were in overdrive—first the murder, then the injury, and of course losing Marisa.

"Do you know if the time travelers left safely?" Katz's questioned the older man.

"What is this time traveler?" confusingly asked his escort.

Mr. Katz you are on a train heading to America…

Munich, Germany-November 8, 1923

These men are the most organized group I have ever seen" thought Ramos.

"Damn I've been around some tough mobsters, but this Aronin team is amazing" mumbled the seasoned Detective.

Within minutes they escorted the time travelers to the lab building, opening doors like they owned the place.

"I guess they have been in this lab before." joked Marisa as they directed them into Dr. Knoeble's office.

Before them stood two wooden lab tables, which were hooked into the transporter, Marisa did not even notice how massive the unit was when she arrived.

The entire room was entangled wires and conductors; it reminded Carlos of a spider's web.

Marisa asked one of the men for a pocket knife, to draw blood.

"Alright Carlos give me your finger" Marisa requested.

"Hell no, I will pass out." responded Ramos.

Marisa carefully placed the blood samples into the glass receiver, it was one of those obsolete microscope slides.

Once the DNA was entered, Marisa fired up the transporter, it was extremely loud, and Aronin's men covered their ears.

Sparks began to fly from the connectors like miniature firework display; Marisa and Carlos rushed get on the transport tables.

Once strapped in, the men attempted to move the giant implementation lever, which resembled a long metal ax hand.

The massive men were straining every muscle fiber to ignite the transporter.

"Stop!" "Stop!" cried out Dr. Knoeble as he stormed into the room.

"I saw the lights from the street." "How dare you break into here." the Doctor continued in a fury.

As Dr. Knoeble angrily reached forward to release Marisa, he fell face first into the electrical current—causing his body to melt into human lava.

As the Doctor melted, behind she could see Aronin bent over and holding his side.

"God be with both of you!" the Mentor cried out.

With a slight push of the hand the lever clicked—the time travelers were gone…

Columbia University-NYC 2008

C lass remember that during muscle contraction—actin and myosin will slide over each other causing the muscle to reduce in size thus contract.

As Professor Williams continued her lesson on the musculoskeletal system, out of the corner of her eye she could see an elderly man enter the room and then sit in back row.

Quietly the man sat as if he was mesmerized by the discussion.

"Class, that is all for today." "We will catch up on Friday." directed the Professor.

Marisa packed up her bag and headed for her next class.

"Wait just a moment." called the voice from the back.

"Sir, may I help you." Marisa inquired.

They both stared into each others eyes; Marisa gave a slight smile in appreciation.

"Let me walk you out." Marisa offered her arm for support.

The gentleman pulled out a ruffled copy of the NY times that was resting under his arm, "such turmoil all the time."

"There is always something going on." Marisa responded.

"Still it is a good world to live in…

www.ingramcontent.com/pod-product-compliance
Lightning Source LLC
Chambersburg PA
CBHW031112260626
47172CB00001B/327